Being Baxters

Being Baxters

KAREN KINGSBURY
and TYLER RUSSELL

A Paula Wiseman Book

Simon & Schuster Books for Young Readers

NEW YORK • LONDON • TORONTO • SYDNEY • NEW DELHI

SIMON & SCHUSTER BOOKS FOR YOUNG READERS
An imprint of Simon & Schuster Children's Publishing Division
1230 Avenue of the Americas, New York, New York 10020

Karen Kingsbury is represented by Alive Communications, Inc.,
8585 Criterion Dr. Unit 63060, Colorado Springs, CO 80920-1045.
Karen Kingsbury is represented by Alive Communications, Inc., 8585 Criterion Dr.
Unit 63060, Colorado Springs, CO 80920-1045.
For information about special discounts for bulk purchases, please contact Simon &
Schuster Special Sales at 1-866-506-1949 or business@simonandschuster.com.
The Simon & Schuster Speakers Bureau can bring authors to your live event. For more
information or to book an event, contact the Simon & Schuster Speakers Bureau at
1-866-248-3049 or visit our website at www.simonspeakers.com.
Interior design by Tom Daly
The text for this book was set in ArrusBT Std.
The illustrations for this book were rendered digitally.
Manufactured in the United States of America
0123 FFG
First Edition
2 4 6 8 10 9 7 5 3 1

Library of Congress Cataloging-in-Publication Data
Names: Kingsbury, Karen, author. | Russell, Tyler, author.
Title: Being Baxters / Karen Kingsbury and Tyler Russell.
Description: First edition. | New York : Simon & Schuster Books for Young Readers, 2023.
| Series: A Baxter family children story ; 5 | "A Paula Wiseman Book." | Audience: Ages
8–12. | Audience: Grades 4–6. | Summary: Each of the Baxter children experiences trouble at
school, and when Principal Bond announces a new Character Awards initiative competition
breaks out between the siblings until they remember what being a Baxter really means.
Identifiers: LCCN 2022043673 (print) | LCCN 2022043674 (ebook) | ISBN
9781665908054 (hardcover) | ISBN 9781665908078 (ebook)
Subjects: CYAC: Family life—Fiction. | Siblings—Fiction. | Schools—Fiction. |
Christian life—Fiction. | LCGFT: Novels.
Classification: LCC PZ7.K6117 Bc 2023 (print) | LCC PZ7.K6117 (ebook) |
DDC [Fic]—dc23
LC record available at https://lccn.loc.gov/2022043673
LC ebook record available at https://lccn.loc.gov/2022043674

To Donald, my love of thirty-three years,
and to my children and grandchildren, life with
you has always been the greatest adventure. From
Austin's baseball games and EJ's soccer matches, to
seeing Kelsey and Tyler in a dozen CYT musicals . . .
through hiking the Arizona mountains and exploring
the Northwest's Columbia Gorge, and now to the
thrill of finding new adventures with our precious
little ones, this life is a gift. I love you always and
forever, and I thank God for you all.
—Karen

To the reader, wherever you are and whatever your
age, may you keep your eyes open to the adventures
that await you. Thank you for reading these stories.
Thank you for your enthusiastic letters, responses,
and support. If no one has told you today, you are
special. To my family, thank you for all the ways you
have blessed my life and for all the adventures we've
had together. Can't wait to see what awaits us in the
chapters ahead. And to my Lord and Savior, Jesus
Christ. All I have and all I do is because of You and
for You. Thank you for giving me stories to share.
I pray I tell them well. Happy reading, friends.
—Tyler

Dear Reader,

As you grow up, you will come to see that character is everything! The way you respect and love your parents and family and your determination to be honest and kind and good will shape the course of your life. So will your ability to help other people, and your decision to be loyal and helpful and to take good care of God's creation and appreciate the things He gives you.

All of that comes down to character.

In Galatians 5, the Bible talks about these characteristics of a person as the fruit of the Spirit—proof that a person is seeking after God's heart. The fruit of the Spirit is love, joy, peace, patience, kindness, goodness, faithfulness, gentleness, and self-control.

In this book you will see how the Baxter children take the journey from grumbly to grateful, and how they remember the very traits that make them one of our favorite families. Through disappointments and the impending doom of a massive blizzard, through frustrations and the funniest moments of all, Brooke, Kari, Ashley, Erin and Luke must remember what it means to be a Baxter.

As you read, we hope you remember what it means to be you, too! Look for ways to shine in the places where

God has you. Because you get just one chance at today, one chance to live your life the best you can. Say something kind, help someone out, smile at that person who needs it most. Seeing someone smile will make you smile, too. Whether at home or at school or church, make every minute count!

Just like the Baxter children do!

Love, Karen
and Tyler

Being Baxters

BROOKE BAXTER—an eighth grader at Bloomington Middle School in Indiana. She is studious and smart and happy about her family's move. Like before, she has her own room.

KARI BAXTER—a sixth grader at Bloomington Elementary School. She is pretty, kind, and ready to make new friends—even if that means starting a new sport. Out in their huge backyard, Kari and Ashley find the perfect meeting spot for the family.

ASHLEY BAXTER—a fifth grader at Bloomington Elementary. When life gets crazy, Ashley is right in the middle of the mess. Always. She is a dreamer and an artist, open to trying new things. She sees art in everything, and is easily the funniest Baxter child.

ERIN BAXTER—a third grader at Bloomington Elementary. She is quiet and soft-spoken, and she loves spending time with their mom. She has her own room in the new house.

LUKE BAXTER—a second grader at Bloomington Elementary. He's good at sports, but sometimes he's a little too risky. Most of all he's happy and hyper. He loves God and his family—especially his sister Ashley.

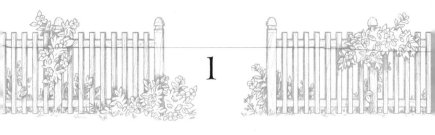

1

Back to the Rock

ASHLEY

The Baxter family children needed a meeting.

That's what Ashley Baxter figured. She sat with her four siblings at the dining room table that Saturday morning, hands cupped around a mug of orange juice. She leaned close to the drink and blew over the top of it. The orange juice rippled just below the rim and splashed over the sides.

Luke stared at her. He was the youngest. "Why do you blow on it?" Luke kneeled on the chair and leaned nearly all the way across the table, using his elbows as supports. "It's not hot."

"It is to me, Luke." Ashley remembered to smile. "It's my own personal almost-coffee. Because I'm in a thinking mood." She patted Luke's head. "You'll understand when you're my age."

Ashley was in fifth grade. Luke was in second. He wouldn't know anything about hard mornings or remembering to smile. But today was especially hard for Ashley for one reason. The same reason they needed a meeting. Two words:

Character and *awards*.

"Ashley." Brooke smiled at her from the kitchen, where she was helping Mom make French toast. "If you think life is hard now, just wait. Middle school is right around the corner."

"No, thank you." Ashley swapped a look with Kari. "We're never growing up, right, Kari?" Kari was in sixth grade, and she and Ashley shared a room. Next year Kari would be in middle school, too.

"That's the deal." Kari nodded. "Never grow up."

Dad walked into the kitchen. "Something smells great!" He hugged Mom and grinned at Brooke. "Another perfect winter Saturday for the Baxter family."

Ashley blew at a wisp of her brown hair. "I'm

2

not sure about that, Dad." She looked at Erin, their younger sister, and then at Brooke and Kari and Luke. "The Baxter kids need a meeting. At the rock. As soon as we finish breakfast."

"As soon as you finish dishes." Mom's eyes smiled at her.

"Right." Ashley gave her mother a thumbs-up. "As soon as we finish dishes."

When the French toast was ready, the whole family sat around the table and Dad prayed. "Thank You, God, for Brooke, Kari, Ashley, Erin, and Luke. They are the kindest, most brave and considerate children I know."

Ashley opened one eyeball and stared at her father. Perhaps he could be their spokesperson to the Bloomington Elementary School character award team.

Her dad was still praying. "Thank You, God, because these kids of ours work together and play together and they do something most siblings don't often do. They have fun together. Thank You for that, and for this food, in Jesus's name, amen."

Ashley jumped to her feet and started to clap.

"Bravo, Dad! Bravo." She looked at her siblings, encouraging them to join her until all five of them were standing and giving their father a rowdy round of applause.

"Why are we clapping?" Brooke looked from Ashley to her parents and back again.

"Because, Brooke." Ashley finally sat back down. Her hands were sore. "At least one person sees who we *really* are. Did you hear his prayer? If that's true, we each should've won a character award at school by now."

Mom raised her eyebrows at Ashley. "We've talked about this."

Kari nodded. "It's true. We have talked about it."

"But . . ." Ashley's next words came very fast. "Maybe we should talk about it again. Maybe Dad should talk about it. To the principal. Because zero character awards for the Baxter children is a tragedy, I tell you. An absolute tragedy."

Her father started to laugh, but he covered his mouth. Because this was no laughing matter, clearly. He reached out and put his hand over hers. "As long as you're winning at home, that's what matters." He looked around. "Speaking of being at home . . . the Farmer's Almanac says there's a massive blizzard headed our way."

Ashley set her fork down. Again, she stood up. "A massive blizzard?" She ran to the window and looked out. The entire sky was bright blue. She looked back at her dad. "Today?"

"No." Dad shook his head. This time he didn't try to cover his laugh. "They're predicting it will hit in early February . . . a few weeks from now."

"Whew." Ashley returned to the table and sat down once more. She looked around. "I can honestly tell you, my fellow family members, that I am not ready for a blizzard."

"Biggest blizzard in a hundred years." Dad took a bite of his French toast. He raised his fork in the air. "That's what the Farmer's Almanac says."

Ashley studied the little bites of French toast swimming in the lake of syrup on her plate. *A Farmer's Almond Hat.* "Does the hat help the farmers know when it's going to snow?"

"The hat?" Brooke wrinkled her nose. "What hat?"

5

"The almond hat." Ashley looked at her mother, then back to Dad. "Isn't that what you said? The farmer's almond hat?"

"Almanac." Her father laughed again.

Ashley did a slight bow. Because apparently she was providing a great deal of humor this morning.

Dad cleared his throat. "The Farmer's Almanac has been printed every year for more than two centuries. Since the late seventeen hundreds. Every year the editors make predictions about weather." He smiled at Mom.

"Yes." Their mother turned to Ashley. "The editors use a secret formula based on solar patterns and historical weather conditions. It's somewhat scientific."

Ashley's entire head was swimming with this new information. "And they think we're having a gigantic blizzard? This year?"

"They do." Dad took another bite of French toast. "Of course, only God knows whether a storm like that will actually happen."

"God doesn't need an almanac for that!" Luke took his plate to the kitchen. "I'll start the dishes."

Everyone was finished eating, so the children sprang into action. Once the dishes were done, they slid into their boots, zipped up their coats and slapped on beanies. Because mid-January in Bloomington, Indiana, was cold as an icebox outside.

When they were ready, all five Baxter kids hurried out the back door. Ashley was the last one.

"Come on, Bo!" Ashley called for their dog. He ran up, his ears flopping and tail wagging. "It's meeting time." She patted his head and ushered him along. Then she shut the door behind her.

There was no snow on the ground today, so Brooke led the way through the forever-long grassy field to the big rock at the far side of their backyard. They pushed past a line of trees and there it was—the stream that ran behind the house. And the rock, of course.

Their own private rock.

Ashley and the others scrambled up onto the top of it. There was room for each of them to sit down. Painted on the top were all of their handprints from when they moved in last summer. Beneath the painted hands were their names.

"Look at this." Luke tried to match his hand to his handprint. "It doesn't line up." He lifted his face to Brooke. "I think the paint is shrinking."

"No." Brooke's smile was a little sad. "Your hand is getting bigger, Luke." She tried to match hers and Ashley could see the same thing. "See? My hand is bigger now, too."

Ashley felt her heart drop. She found her handprint and tried to line up her hand over it. Brooke was right. Her hand didn't fit there now, either. It was happening.

They were growing up. Despite their promise.

A chilly quiet came over the five of them. Ashley lifted her hand from the painted one on the rock. It was time to think about something else.

From a nearby tree, an owl let out a long *hooo-hoo*. The wind whistled through the bare branches above them. Bo panted and a flock of birds flew by overhead.

"Do you hear that?" Ashley smiled at her siblings. "It's a beautiful winter symphony." She raised her ear toward the sky. "And it's saying not to worry about growing up. Not today."

The others nodded. "I like that." Brooke settled into her spot. "Let's have our meeting. It's freezing out here."

"You have a point." Ashley's teeth were starting to chatter. "Okay. The meeting is about the failed character awards."

Luke shrugged. "It wasn't a fail for everyone. Lots of kids have won certificates."

"Well, it's been a fail for us." Ashley scooted next to Kari. "Get closer. Everyone. So we don't fall to hyperthermia."

"Hypothermia. Hyperthermia is when you're too hot." Brooke slid closer to Erin and Luke. "Ashley's right. Shoulder to shoulder, people."

When they were huddled together, Ashley took a deep breath. "The thing is, we need a plan if we're going to win a character award."

"Like a strategy?" Kari blinked. She was shivering a little.

"Exactly." Ashley put her arm around Kari's shoulders. "A strategy. Which is why I'm thinking I should coach us. You know, like lessons where we meet each week and practice some new skills. Like training for the basketball team. Or the Army."

"Training?" Erin shook her head. "I think Mom is right. We just have to keep doing our best."

"At least you have character awards." Brooke leaned in closer to the others. "In middle school you just do your work and stay quiet."

Ashley shuddered. That sounded terrible. "We only have this one chance." She swapped looks with Kari and Erin and Luke. And suddenly she felt a stirring inside her. Beneath her ribs. Or maybe that was the French toast.

Either way, before she could stop herself, she jumped up and threw her hands in the air. "Training! Yes, that's exactly what we're going to do." Ashley dropped back down to the rock and squeezed in tight with the others. "We will train. We will strategize. We will learn how to be the kinds of students Principal Bond wants." She snapped her fingers a few times. "What was it Principal Bond wanted? Do you remember?"

"Honesty." Kari nodded. "I remember that."

"And respect." Luke pointed at Ashley. "Always be respectful."

"Okay." Ashley felt her heart beat faster. "Now we're getting somewhere."

"What about cooperation?" Erin looked from Luke to Ashley. "He talks about that a lot."

"Good job, Erin!" Ashley high-fived her youngest sister. "Definitely cooperation."

"So how will we train for that?" Luke seemed ready to start the program.

Ashley's mind raced. "Well . . . how about this: I will develop a strategy, lessons. Ways we can practice." She tapped her chin. "It'll be a Baxter playbook."

"I don't know, Ashley." Kari shook her head. "This feels like the wrong way to do it."

"Have I ever led you wrong?" Ashley held her hands open. "I'm as reliable as the farmer's almond hat."

"Almanac." Brooke giggled.

"Right. That." Ashley helped her siblings to their feet. "Trust me. If we do this right, each of us could win a character award before spring break. That gives us two months." Ashley held out her hands. "Come on. Make a circle."

They all held hands.

"I'm freezing." Erin shivered hard. "Fine, Ashley. You can be our coach."

"We'll meet in Luke's room and start this afternoon." A sharp breeze cut through Ashley's winter coat. "But first . . . hot chocolate!"

They put their hands in the middle then and Brooke counted them out. "One-two-three . . ."

And all together—like they'd done every time they came to the rock lately—the Baxter children shouted out loud, "Baxters!"

Ashley led the way as they scrambled off the rock. The chilly air poked pins at their cheeks, but once they were back inside Mom had five mugs of steaming hot chocolate lined up in a row.

"What's a winter rock meeting without hot chocolate?" Mom grinned at them. "How did it go?"

Ashley raised her eyebrows. "We shall see, Mother. We shall see."

Long after they had finished their drinks, Ashley sat by the fireplace drawing. She placed herself in front of her four siblings, whistle around her neck. Very soon, training would begin. Brooke might as well join them. She wouldn't win any awards, but at least she'd impress her teachers. That had to count for something.

Yes, Ashley would come up with a list of drills and exercises to help them win a character award. Each of them, if she had anything to do with it.

Because the Baxters had what it took to be winners.

Ashley was sure.

2

An Unusually Emotional Afternoon

KARI

Kari's mind was on one thing—the character award assembly happening when PE was over. But first she had to finish the last few minutes of sixth-grade basketball.

The PE assignment was simple, at least for most kids in her class. Catch a pass, dribble four times, and make a basket. A close-up basket. A layup.

Do that and Kari would pass the basketball unit. But so far, every time Kari shot the ball, it hadn't even hit the rim. This was her last chance.

Kari had fallen asleep last night praying she would pass.

"Okay, Kari, it's your turn." Their PE teacher, Mr. Stone, nodded. "You can do it."

"Yes, sir." Kari stared at the basketball hoop. The voices of her classmates and the sound of a dozen bouncing basketballs all grew dim until the only thing Kari could hear was the beat of her heart.

Ba-boom. Ba-boom. Ba-boom.

Kari's forehead felt sweaty. She looked at Mandy. "Okay," she yelled out. "Ready!"

"You got this." Mandy dribbled the ball twice. "Here you go!"

With that, Mandy passed the ball across the court to Kari. It seemed to sail through the air in slow motion, and this time with confident hands, Kari caught it. She actually did. *Yes,* she thought. *A good start.* Then she dribbled four times without hitting her feet or losing the ball. *Also good,* she told herself.

Finally, she raised the ball up over her head, just the way Mr. Stone had taught them. It felt heavy, like a bowling ball. But this time Kari shot it up toward the basket and . . .

Swish!

The basketball dropped through the net and bounced on the hardwood floor. Kari stood frozen for a moment, but then she released the longest breath. She had passed! The ball had gone in!

"You did it, Kari!" Mr. Stone clapped and so did the other students in Kari's class.

"Look at you go, girl!" Liza's voice echoed through the gym.

"I knew you could do it!" Mandy ran to Kari and hugged her. Then she took Kari's hand and held it up. Like Kari had won gold in the Olympics.

Ten minutes later, their teacher, Ms. Nan, entered the gym and took a seat in the bleachers. Kari and the rest of her class joined her. And soon every boy and girl was gathered in their assigned seats in the gym.

It was time for the character award assembly.

Kari took a deep breath. She didn't want to get her hopes up. Ashley's class happened to sit right next to Kari's. So Kari shifted her way over until she sat right next to Ashley. Kari leaned close and whispered, "Maybe today's the day."

"We haven't started our official training." Ashley clenched her teeth. "But yes, maybe today. I am not holding my breath here. Plus my report on deserts was not a win."

"What happened?" Kari frowned. The other kids were still taking their places, so for now they could talk.

Ashley shrugged. "Apparently it's the Mo-hav-ee desert. I said Mo-*jave*." Ashley covered her face with one hand and shook her head. "A silent *j*. Who knew?"

Kari couldn't help but laugh. If there was an award for most entertaining, Ashley would've won it, hands down.

Principal Bond walked up to the podium. "Hello, boys and girls! We have exciting news about the book fair, but first, this week's character awards!"

Ashley linked arms with Kari and squeezed tight.

"Everyone settle down, please." The principal waited. A few rounds of *shhhs* made their way across the gym until finally it was quiet. "Thank you." He looked around the packed room.

Kari and Ashley stayed stone still, waiting.

"The faculty and I have been very impressed with the environment of the school since introducing the character awards back in December." Principal Bond smiled a friendly smile. "We have seen our community become more caring, more respectful, and more helpful. As your principal, I am very proud of your efforts." He looked at a sheet of paper in his hand. "And with that . . . on to our winners."

Suddenly Ashley released Kari's arm. And before Kari could stop her, Ashley stood straight up and raised her hand. The entire school turned and stared at her.

"The first award goes to—" The principal looked up and stopped midsentence. He aimed his eyeballs straight at Ashley. "Miss Baxter? Is there a problem?"

Ashley spoke loud enough for the principal and everyone else to hear. "Hello, sir. No, no problem. Just wondering." She smiled. "How does this whole character award thing work?"

Principal Bond blinked.

"You know . . ." Ashley continued. "Who keeps score? Who's watching? Are there spies in the hallways? Or cameras?" Ashley hesitated. "We need to know these things."

Kari slumped down in her seat. On the other

side, Mandy's mouth hung open. Liza's, too. Silence filled the gym. "Ashley." Kari used her loudest whisper. She tugged on her sister's sweater. "Sit down!"

But Ashley stayed standing, eyes locked on the principal. "Take your time, sir." She smiled again, patient.

The principal seemed a little shocked. He raised his eyebrows up into his forehead. "Miss Baxter. There are no spies. No cameras. The teachers nominate students based on their character. That's how it works." He paused. "Please sit down."

Ashley glanced at Mr. Garrett, her teacher. The man was standing at the opposite side of her row. He did not look happy. He motioned to Ashley. "Sit down now!"

Kari shook her head. Her sister had really done it this time. She tried pulling Ashley down again. "Ashley, come on."

Ashley looked down at Kari, then back at Mr. Bond. It must have hit her what she had done. "My apologies." Ashley did a formal bow. "As you were, Principal Bond." Then, finally, she sat down.

"Thank you, Ashley. Now . . ." The principal held the paper back up. "This week's character awards . . ."

Principal Bond read off name after name and handed out award after award. Through it all, Kari could still feel their classmates looking at Ashley.

And, once again, not a single award went to any of the Baxter children.

That afternoon while Kari and her siblings did homework at the kitchen table, Kari still felt disappointed about the awards. "Ashley's right." She looked at the others. "We need training."

Ashley tapped her chin a few times. "And so we shall get it." She stared at Kari. "It has to be spies. How else do they know who's good and who's not?"

"Probably just . . . intuition." Kari thought about her teacher. "Adults know a lot of things just by being adults."

"*Into-what?* That's a really big word." Luke was writing out his math problems. "What's it mean?"

"It's a spelling word this week." Kari pulled her homework out of her backpack.

Ashley looked at Kari. "How do you spell it?"

"Ask me on Friday." Kari laughed. She had just gotten the list, so she wasn't exactly an expert.

Mom came to the table with a tray of apple slices and string cheese. "I know it's disappointing, but just be patient with the awards. Keep being you. If it's meant to happen, it'll happen."

"Ashley asked the principal how awards were decided." Luke smiled. "Nice one, Ash."

A frown came over Mom's face. She turned to Ashley. "You what?"

"I stood up, raised my hand and asked." Ashley smiled. "Very polite, of course." She took a quick breath. "Didn't get a real answer."

Mom gave Ashley a look but before she could say anything Ashley shook her head. "That wasn't the lowlight of my day, though. The saddest lowlight was Mr. Garrett's announcement."

Erin was writing in her composition book. She stopped and turned to Ashley. "What announcement?"

"In the saddest news of all time, Mr. Garrett told us he is not coming back to school for a

21

month. Starting tomorrow. On a Tuesday, of all things."

"He's quitting?" Luke wrinkled his nose. "In the middle of the year?"

"No." Ashley sighed. "He is going home to be with his wife. Apparently, she's having a baby this week. Which means a substitute teacher for me." She raised her hands and dropped them, very dramatic. "An entire four whole weeks."

"A baby? How wonderful." Mom leaned back in her chair.

Kari wondered if their mother had forgotten about Ashley and the principal.

"Not wonderful." Ashley frowned. "Not for us. Mr. Garrett is the best teacher in the world." She nibbled at an apple slice. "Let's hope the substitute is a good one."

"Yes." Mom sighed. "I substituted once. For a short season." She smiled, as if happy memories were coming back. "Such a lovely time."

"Like . . . when you were shorter?" Ashley looked confused.

Mom laughed. "No, Ashley . . . for a small

amount of time . . . a short time. Just a few months after college. But I had fun. And I can promise you the substitute, whoever he or she is, will be just as nervous as you are."

"We'll see about that." Ashley took another few bites of her apples.

Kari took two slices for her plate. "I'm sure the substitute will be fine." She patted Ashley's hand. "Mr. Garrett would only pick a good one."

"You have a point." Ashley looked hopeful.

"Well." Mom grinned at Kari. "I have some good news. I spoke with your dance teacher today, Kari. She has assigned you a solo for the upcoming recital!"

"Really?" Kari felt her heart beat faster. She sat up a little straighter. A solo and a basketball shot in the same afternoon? Character awards or not, this was turning out to be a good day.

"Yay, Kari!" Ashley stood and danced in a few circles. "If you need tips, let me know. I don't want to brag. But I'm a pretty good dancer." She stopped and did three spins, punching her arms in the air with each one.

23

"Nice!" Kari high-fived Ashley. "Definitely. Something like that."

Just then they heard the front door open and then slam again in a hurry.

"Brooke? Is that you?" Mom hurried toward the front door.

"That didn't sound good." Kari gave Ashley a worried look.

Ashley kept her eyes on the hallway toward the front door. "Let's go see." She slid out of her chair and tiptoed for the door.

Kari followed her sister down the hallway. There they saw Brooke and Mom sitting on the first step of the staircase. Mom had her arm around Brooke.

"It's just so unfair." Brooke sniffled. "I didn't do anything."

"Sometimes people exclude us for no reason. One day they love you, the next they won't look at you." Mom pulled Brooke in closer. "It doesn't make it easy."

"What happened?" Kari took a few steps toward Mom and Brooke. Ashley followed a few feet behind.

Mom looked at Brooke. "Can I tell them?"

Brooke was too emotional to speak. She nodded her head.

The story spilled out. One of Brooke's friends, Ella, stopped including Brooke at lunchtime. For no reason.

Kari couldn't believe it. She sat next to Brooke and put her head on her big sister's shoulder. "You can always sit with me, Brooke," Kari whispered.

Brooke let out a long exhale. "Thanks, Kari."

Ashley crossed her arms. "Who is this Ella girl, anyway? Maybe I can go to your school and teach her a thing or two about manners." Ashley rolled up her sleeves. "I've been taking notes. For the character awards."

"We're not going to teach anyone a lesson." Mom was quick to chime in. "Ella is obviously going through something of her own. It's very sad to feel excluded. But our confidence and joy can't come from what others think of us."

"Where does it come from then?" Kari looked at Mom.

By now, Luke and Erin had joined them. They took seats on the floor.

Mom's voice was kind. "It comes from knowing that you're loved. By God and by those who know you most. You are unique and you have something to offer this world. And no one can change that." Mom took her time, looking at each of the children.

"Not even Ella." Ashley plugged her nose.

Mom smiled. "Right. Not even her."

Just then the door opened and Dad walked in. "This is an interesting place for a family meeting." He looked at each of the kids, then at Mom. "Everything okay?"

"We'll tell you all about it over dinner." Mom stood and helped Kari, Ashley, and Brooke to their feet. Erin and Luke stood, too, and the whole family walked back to the kitchen.

Only then did Dad share his news. "Dr. Cohen called." He looked at Erin. "He said it was a good thing we brought you in last week. I'm afraid you have to have glasses, honey."

Erin's eyes filled with tears. "No, thank you."

"I'm sorry, Erin. You really need them." Dad pulled her into a hug.

"But . . ." Erin's voice cracked. "Everyone is gonna call me *four eyes*." Erin turned and melted into Mother's arms.

"No one is going to call you that." Mom wiped at the tears rolling down Erin's cheeks.

Kari blinked. So many tears today. Definitely unusual for a Baxter family afternoon.

Luke patted Erin's back. "It's okay, Erin. Glasses make you look smart."

"But . . ." Erin sniffled. "I already am smart."

Luke had no response. From her spot on the stair, Kari watched Luke look for help.

"Listen to me, Erin." Ashley walked over and joined the growing group hug, trying to support Luke's thought. "What Luke means is it's nice to look smart. When you are smart. Which . . . you are."

The family formed a group hug. Kari joined in with the others. "You will look so cute in glasses, Erin. I promise." She squeezed Erin tight.

"True." Erin let out a long sigh. "All right, then. I'm hungry."

Mom laughed. "What about you, Luke? Any news today?"

"Yes!" He jumped a few times, like he had only just now remembered. "My class is going on a field trip! To see the Harlem Globetrotters!"

Ashley gasped. "No way! That is the most fun thing." She hesitated. "What is it?"

Dad held out a pretend basketball. "Picture this." He rolled the invisible ball down his back, caught it, and swung it around his waist. "The Globetrotters can do just about anything with a basketball." Their father winced. "Let's hope the Farmer's Almanac is wrong. Or else the blizzard could be a problem for your field trip."

"Let's hope those farmers are wrong." Luke scowled. "I don't wanna miss my field trip."

"Yes, I meant to ask." Ashley put her hands on her hips. "What if we get buried in snow?"

Kari patted her sister's arm. "I don't think that will happen."

"At least then I wouldn't have to see Ella." Brooke shrugged. She looked happier than before.

"And my class wouldn't have to see me with

glasses." Erin linked arms with Brooke.

While Mom and Dad finished dinner, Kari found her journal. She had a lot on her mind as she began to write.

Hello. It's me. Dad says a huge storm is coming. Except I have a big dance solo, and Luke has a field trip, and we are trying to win character awards. So, this might not be the best time for a storm. Also, Ashley and Brooke and Erin are kind of sad today. I wish I could give them a character award. They don't deserve to be sad. I hope they know how much God loves them. It's almost dinnertime. More later! Kari.

3

The Very Terrible Substitute Situation

ASHLEY

Ashley felt sick.

The seatbelt was choking her. She loosened it and fumbled with the air-conditioning on the car ceiling. Outside it was freezing, but here on the way to school, hot air gathered around Ashley's mouth and made it hard to breathe.

And they were only halfway to school.

Nervous sweat drops ran down her forehead. She wasn't sick. No, it was something much worse. Today she was going to meet Mr. Garrett's substitute teacher.

Yesterday Mr. Garrett canceled the lesson plan and gave the class Red Vines licorice and caramel corn and they played games and listened to the Beach Boys. It was one for the books. That's what Mr. Garrett said. Only now the truth was actually sinking in.

Mr. Garrett was gone.

A kind of bubbly scared feeling made its way through Ashley. She'd never known school without Mr. Garrett. From the first day they met, when Ashley had dropped ice cream on his head, her teacher had been as dependable as an ocean wave. Always there.

He was her first friend at this school.

Dad was dropping them off today. Ashley pressed against the seatbelt and leaned forward. "How about I spend the day with you? At the hospital."

Their father was a doctor. He looked at Ashley in the rearview mirror. "I thought you didn't like the hospital."

"True. Career Day was not my greatest highlight. But maybe I need to give it another shot." Ashley fumbled with the seatbelt again. It kept getting tighter.

"Ah, I get it." Dad pulled up at the front of the school and smiled back at Ashley. "This is about the substitute teacher."

The other kids waved goodbye to Dad and climbed out.

But Ashley's heart pounded like a giant drum. Her throat closed a little. "But . . . I'm really going to miss Mr. Garrett." She barely got the words out. She didn't want to cry. She wouldn't let it happen. She closed her eyes and took a few breaths.

Dad patted her shoulder. "Ashley. Change is hard. But give it a try. Your substitute could be amazing. Remember our Bible story?"

The words came back to her. Ashley swallowed the lump in her throat. "Be strong . . . and courageous." She felt herself relax a bit.

"That's right, Ashley." Dad squeezed her hand. "God is with you wherever you go."

Ashley unbuckled her seatbelt. "I hope someone told the substitute that."

She hugged Dad and, moving slower than usual, she stepped out of the car. Her friends Elliot and Landon and Natalie were just ahead of her. "Hey, wait!" she called out and then ran to catch up.

The four of them walked together to their class-room. Along the way Elliot talked about a new book he was reading. One about aliens. He was the only one in their group of friends who liked space beings.

But he also liked their group of friends. And that's what mattered.

They got to the room and set their backpacks and coats on the classroom hooks. Ashley looked around. She saw their principal in the corner of the room. Surely, he wasn't the substitute.

"I wonder who the sub's gonna be." Landon stood beside Ashley. "Can't be Principal Bond."

"Definitely not." Ashley looked at Landon. "But at least we know him."

"True." Landon tossed his hair to one side. "It's like the first day of school all over again."

"I thought the same thing." Ashley sighed. "Glad to know I'm not alone."

"And I'm glad to see you brought normal shoes to school today." Landon chuckled in Ashley's direction.

"Thank you very much." Ashley laughed, too. Landon was talking about the time Ashley brought ballet shoes to science camp and she had to wear Landon's extra shoes. Shoes that were way too big for Ashley.

It made for a silly memory.

Landon was a good friend. What kind of guy offers up their own shoes for someone else? Landon Blake—that's who. If he was here, along with Elliot and Natalie, then Ashley would be okay, whoever the substitute turned out to be.

The bell rang and everyone hurried to their seats. There was no extra chatter. Clearly, everyone was thinking about the substitute.

At that very moment the door flung open.

One girl in the back row screamed. Maybe because of the speed of the door or possibly because of the sight of the person bursting through. A ripple of gasps filtered across the room.

A skinny woman, maybe eight feet tall, lurched through the door, slumped over a large stack of papers in her arms. Hanging from her neck was a pair of glasses.

Later Elliot would say the woman had a sort of alien-like space beauty.

Ashley couldn't stop staring. She wasn't sure if she should be amazed or terrified. She felt a little bit of both.

Never before had the class been so quiet.

The woman strutted to Mr. Garrett's desk and turned to Principal Bond.

"Class." The principal smiled. "This is Ms. Stritch. She will be your substitute teacher while Mr. Garrett is away."

Now the woman turned to the blackboard. With a piece of white chalk, she wrote her name: *Ms. Stritch*. Then she turned to Principal Bond. "Thank you." She had a British accent. "I can take it from here."

In a blur, the principal left and Ashley, Natalie, Elliot, Landon and their classmates were all alone with Ms. Stritch.

For a minute, the woman sorted through her papers while the class stared.

Ms. Stritch's blond hair was pulled back in a bun that sat tight at the back of her head. Like a lemon. Not a strand was out of place. Her cheek-bones jetted out like sharp points, cartoon-style. She wore a black skirt that went all the way to her ankles and her gray turtleneck stretched up to her chin. As she walked closer to the students, her heels *click-clack-clicked* on the floor and her skirt flowed every which way.

I will definitely be drawing a picture of this woman later, Ashley thought to herself.

Ms. Stritch faced the class and the corner of her mouth lifted ever so slightly. Almost a smile. Or maybe she was holding in a secret or a sneeze. Either way, Ashley sat frozen at her desk. She didn't want to breathe too loud.

This woman was the most interesting person she'd ever seen.

And not entirely in a good way.

"Thank you for being quiet, class." The substitute stared them down. "As your principal said, I am Ms. Stritch. I am an educator from London, and I am finishing up my master's degree at Indiana University."

"Go Hoosiers!" In the second row, Chris—

Landon's friend—threw his fist in the air and made a loud *woo* noise. He looked around for more hearty cheers from the others. But they never came. He dropped his fist.

"What is your name, boy?" Ms. Stritch stared at Chris.

Chris seemed a little paler than before. He slipped down in his chair some. "Chris. Just making you feel welcome."

"Yes." Ms. Stritch did not smile. "Thank you for that, Chris."

Words were trying to get out of Ashley's mouth. She pressed her lips together, but it was no use and finally she stood and waved at Ms. Stritch. "I'm Ashley Baxter, and I'd just like to say, G'day, mate!"

Ashley flashed a huge smile and sat back down.

"Excuse me?" Ms. Stritch stared at her.

Ashley's cheeks felt suddenly hot, as if the substitute's vision rays were perhaps actually laser beams.

Maybe the woman didn't understand. Ashley cleared her throat. "You know, cause of the accent.

G'day, mate! You're British, right?"

"Ashley. That is an Australian saying." Again Ms. Stritch did not crack a smile. "Brits are from England."

"Okay, then." Ashley stood again. She raised an invisible hat in the air. Then she did a spin. "Cheeri-ho! And enjoy some tea and crumpets!" Ashley struck a pose with the invisible hat, waiting for Ms. Stritch to laugh. Or smile. But she did neither.

"That's closer." Ms. Stritch motioned for Ashley to take her seat. "Please sit."

Ashley slumped down to her chair. Even her close friends were staring at her.

Apparently, Ms. Stritch was going to be a tough woman to crack.

"Ms. Stritch." Natalie raised her hand and stood up. "Welcome to class. We usually begin with roll call and then the word of the day."

Elliot raised his hand. "Or the joke of the day. Sometimes it's a joke."

"No. He's kidding." Natalie rolled her eyes. "We don't do jokes."

"But we could." Chris chimed in. "Like this

one: What lights up a stadium?" Chris paused and then held his arms out for dramatic flair. "A soccer match." He paused. "Get it? A soccer match because a match can really light up a place."

Ms. Stritch did not smile or blink or say a word. Instead she slid her long arms behind her back and rocked forward on her feet. "I shall wait." She looked hard at the class.

And so the teacher waited, her hands behind her back. She didn't have to say anything. Her presence told the students everything they needed to know.

The substitute did not want noise. And she meant business.

Within seconds the class fell quiet. So quiet Ashley could hear her nose breaths.

Ms. Stritch took a deep breath. "Now," she said. "I don't know how you do things with Mr. Garrett, nor do I care. This is my classroom now. I am well-equipped to teach and I don't need any suggestions. We do not blurt out during class. And we do not take charge. That is my job." She looked at Ashley, then at Chris. Then she continued. "We listen until spoken to. Understood?"

A few mumbles came from the class in response.

The substitute came a step closer. "I said . . . *understood?*" She said the word louder this time.

"Yes, ma'am." This time, everyone responded at the same time.

Ashley's eyes had grown wider than they'd ever been in all her life. She slid down a little lower in her seat. Her chin was almost on her desk. Anything to keep from being noticed again.

"Very well." Ms. Stritch returned to the blackboard. "We will begin with the word of the day. A word from your spelling list." Ms. Stritch scribbled the word on the board. "*Ominous.*" She spun around and studied them. Then back to the board. "*O-M-I-N-O-U-S.*"

Ashley wasn't sure what the word meant. But she didn't like the sound of it. She wished for Ms. Stritch to turn around and say, "*Just kidding!*" But that didn't happen.

Ms. Stritch walked closer to the class again. "Does anyone know what *ominous* means?"

Ashley had an idea. When a group of people hum, and the leader of the group explains the situation.

Sort of like a hum in us. But she didn't dare say so.

When no one answered, Ms. Stritch opened her mouth. "*Ominous* means the impression that something bad or unpleasant is going to happen." She hesitated. "Who can use it in a sentence?"

Chris raised his hand. "Mr. Garrett's class felt ominous about him leaving."

Ms. Stritch raised her eyebrows. She thought for a long moment, then she nodded. "Yes. That could work."

Ashley wanted to cheer for Chris, because that was exactly ominous. The whole morning had been ominous. But she stayed quiet.

Recess couldn't come soon enough.

When they were finally outside, Ashley sat on the swings next to Natalie. Ashley kept her swing at a slow pace to match her enthusiasm for this day. "I do believe—with all my heart—that our situation is ominous." Ashley glanced at Natalie.

"Maybe this is a bad dream," Elliot shouted from two swings down. "I read about that in a fantasy book once. Everyone had the same bad dream." Elliot pushed his feet up higher. He was the highest swinger in fifth grade. Because he liked to swing as close to outer space as possible.

"We're all having the same bad dream?" Ashley shook her head. "Not likely, Elliot."

"You could always pinch yourself and see if you wake up." Natalie was a medium swinger. She slowed down to Ashley's pace.

"No thanks. I'm not much of a pincher." Ashley watched Natalie jump off her swing and walk to a patch of grass. She laid down and stared at the sky. Ashley frowned. Over all, Natalie did not seem too concerned about this very terrible substitute situation.

Ashley and Elliot joined Natalie on the soft grass. Ashley picked at a few bright green blades. "We need a plan."

Elliot pushed his glasses back up onto his nose. "What are we supposed to do?"

An idea hit Ashley. "We could switch schools!" She stared at the street that ran alongside the playground. "We could hit the road and find a school across town." Ashley pictured them setting off to find a new school. Adventure on the horizon. A new teacher in their view. Walking all that way. Without food or water.

All alone.

The idea was starting to lose its charm.

"I don't know any other schools." Natalie sat up again.

Elliot was picking at the grass now, too. "I have a theory. I think Ms. Stritch is actually a robot teacher." His eyes got big. "Did you see how she walked? So tall and stiff. She didn't even smile

once." He thought for a moment. "But she was pretty."

"Maybe we'll learn from her. She seems serious." Natalie shook her head. "Besides, there is no such thing as a robot teacher."

"I think there is." Elliot lowered his voice. "They have excellent hearing."

"What do you know about robot teachers?" Ashley kept her voice to a low whisper.

"They're new." Elliot leaned closer to the girls. "They are government robot teachers, sent to spy on us kids. And then they report back to the FBI secret agents. They never laugh, they only eat vegetables, and they force their students to write out spelling words hundreds of times."

"Secret agents." Ashley yelled out the words. Then she covered her mouth and found her whisper again. "I knew our school was using spies. Because of the character awards. We must have a dozen robot teachers at Bloomington Elementary." Ashley gasped. "It all makes sense. She must be a robot."

"No. No way." Natalie crossed her arms. "She's a regular person."

The bell rang and Ashley and her friends stood and faced the school. The classroom door opened and Ms. Stritch stepped outside. She seemed like the least regular person Ashley had ever seen.

"Time will tell." Elliot used his normal voice again.

Ms. Stritch blew a whistle and waited. She was good at waiting, apparently. Ashley and her friends ran back to the classroom and hurried to their seats. During free reading, Ashley took a moment to draw herself in a chair, all alone in the classroom. And Ms. Stritch at the front of the room with a face like a secret spy. Under the drawing, Ashley wrote one word.

Ominous.

Because with every passing hour, Ashley was starting to believe Elliot was right.

Ms. Stritch truly was a robot teacher.

4

Posture on the Prairie

KARI

The first training session for character awards wasn't going very well.

Kari stood with Erin and Luke in a half circle in the living room. Brooke was still at school. *Good for her,* Kari thought. She crossed her arms and looked straight at Ashley. "How is this helping?" Kari tried to keep her tone kind.

"It is, Kari." Ashley came closer and patted Kari's head. "Trust me."

Ashley stood at the front of the group. She held an open notebook in one hand and a pencil in the other. Despite her bad day with her substitute teacher—which they had all heard about on the ride home—Ashley was now completely focused on getting everyone in perfect shape for the awards.

She clapped her hands together. "You should all stand taller. Like there's a book on your head." Ashley demonstrated. Her neck stretched up to the sky. She looked a bit like a giraffe.

"I don't know." Kari tried it, but as she did, she heard something inside her neck crack. "Ow!"

"That was loud!" Luke laughed. "Are you okay?"

"I think so." Kari turned her head one way, then the other. "I don't think cracking my neck is going to help anything." She started to laugh. Because this was a little ridiculous, after all.

"I don't want my neck to pop." Erin looked concerned.

"Hm." Kari exhaled. "I actually feel better."

Ashley frowned at them. "People, you need to focus!" She settled them down.

"So we need to stand tall?" Luke scrunched up his face. "That's going to win us a character award?"

"Yes." Ashley gave her brother a look. "I've been watching the winners. Plus, I'm your coach, Luke. You have to listen to me."

"Fine." Luke shrugged. Kari thought their brother's

eyes looked like they wanted to laugh.

"Very well." Ashley smoothed out her sweater. "Next, we will practice a character award greeting." She took a moment, then she bowed sharply at the waist. "You will either bow like this." She looked at her siblings and gave each of them a friendly nod. "Or you will nod like that." Ashley demonstrated again. "That's what the winners do. I saw for myself."

"How do you know this?" Luke bent at the waist, trying to practice his bow. "What do you think, Ash?"

Ashley studied him. "You have potential, Luke. I can say that for sure."

At that, Erin started nodding at each of them. Three times apiece, until she wobbled a bit. "Like this?" She looked dizzy.

Ashley smiled. "I believe you are definitely getting it, Erin."

Kari started to laugh, but she covered her mouth. "Walking tall? Bowing and nodding?" She tried to be serious, especially since Ashley was. But even so, her laughter came.

"This is not a funny situation." Ashley turned to Kari. She lifted her chin. "Are you serious about winning a character award or not?"

"Yes. I'm serious." Kari covered her mouth and after a few seconds she had her laughter under control. "Go on."

"I will, thank you." Ashley picked up a very used-looking book from a nearby chair. The pages had frayed gold edges. Ashley held it out like a gift. "This book is from the school library." She paused, as if whatever she was about to say held a very great secret. "It is a book on etiquette by Emily Post." Ashley paused. "And let me tell you, this Emily girl was famous for winning character awards."

"Ashley, that book looks a hundred years old." Kari was still trying not to laugh. She crossed her arms again. "What can Emily Post teach us?"

Ashley set the book back down. "She can teach us to stand tall, bow at the waist, and nod our heads, for one thing."

"That's three things." Luke grinned.

"True." Kari shifted in place. She had homework

to get to. "Three things no one does. No one our age." Kari groaned.

"Yeah." Erin rubbed her neck. "Are you sure this is going to work, Ash? I don't get it."

"That's the point, Erin. We will stand out." Ashley checked her notebook and the list of items to review. "We need to work on vocabulary. Practice saying something nice like . . . 'How do you do?' Or 'Thank you, kindly.' Or 'Mighty fine day, ain't it?' Things like that."

"You got that from Emily Post?"

"Well." Ashley squirmed a bit. "Actually. That came from *Little House on the Prairie*. But those kids would've won character awards all day long." She looked around the half circle. "They would have."

"*Mighty fine day?*" Kari giggled again. "Ashley, come on."

Luke raised his hand. "I don't think we should be talking like people on the prairie at school."

Kari had to agree. "Maybe we should pick a more popular show."

"No, no, no." Ashley waved her arms around. "Everyone, listen! What we've been doing hasn't

50

worked. We need a new approach and I personally think Emily Post and *Little House on the Prairie* are the exact right tools to help us."

Kari, Erin and Luke stood there. No one seemed to know what to say.

"Okay. Well. Enough talking." Ashley clapped her hands. "Let's practice." She paced in front of the other three. "Stand tall."

All at once, Kari, Erin, and Luke stood as straight as fence posts.

"Very nice." Ashley paced some more. "Next, bow at the waist and nod your heads. Make eye contact, people. Eye contact counts ten points."

Kari and the others did as they were told, bowing and nodding and standing tall.

"Good. I like it." Ashley stopped pacing and looked at them. "Now let's hear your greetings."

"Thank you, kindly!" Luke bowed at Ashley.

She returned the bow. "Mighty fine day, ain't it?"

Kari stepped up. "How do you do?"

"And ain't it a bee-u-tee-full day?" Erin stretched her neck, but then she made a face. "Ouch. I don't like that stretchy part."

"Erin!" Ashley raised her voice. "Toughen up, here. No whining!"

Suddenly Kari was aware of something. She turned toward the doorway, and there stood Mom. "What is all this?" She took a few steps closer. "What's happening here? And, Ashley, why are you yelling?"

Kari was the first to speak. "We're . . . practicing. For the character awards." She folded her hands. "Personally, I don't think I have what it takes."

"Says who?" Their mother looked at Ashley. "Is this your idea, young lady? The bowing and nodding and . . . the things you four were saying?"

"In fact, it was my idea." Ashley smiled. "And here's the thing, Mother. A good coach sometimes needs to talk loud to her athletes."

"Ashley." Mom's voice was stern, but kind. "Your siblings are not your athletes."

"But . . ." Ashley's posture melted some. "You don't understand. I really, really want us to win." Ashley dropped to the chair next to the Emily Post book. She held it up. "I'm really trying here."

Their mother seemed to relax a little. "I understand that." She shook her head. "But this . . . this coaching is not how you win a character award." She looked from Ashley to Kari and then to Erin and Luke. "No more coaching, Ashley. You do have to work on it, but not like this."

She kissed Erin on the top of her head. "I hope your neck is okay."

Erin rubbed it again. "It's getting better."

Mom looked at Ashley. "I'm going to put away the groceries. You, missy, can get to your homework." She glanced at the others. "You three, too."

When their mother was gone, Ashley sighed. Then in a whispery voice she said, "Please. Just try it. Can we agree to that?"

One at a time, starting with Kari, the three of them nodded. They would try it.

Just to see if Emily Post and Laura Ingalls Wilder were right.

Kari had been practicing for character awards since she walked through the door of school that morning, and now it was lunchtime. She set her food tray down on her usual table just as Liza and

Mandy walked up with theirs. "Hello, ladies." Kari bowed at the waist and smiled at her two friends. "Mighty fine day, ain't it?"

Before her friends could say anything, one of the lunchroom assistants walked by. Kari bowed again. "Good day, ma'am."

The woman hesitated. Then she, too, bent deep at the waist, returning the gesture. "Good day to you." She gave Kari a confused look and continued cleaning the tabletops.

"Kari?" Liza squinted her eyes. "What's going on?"

"Nothing." Kari took a seat, slow and careful. She kept her back as straight as a board.

Mandy took a sip of her juice and giggled. "Really? Cause you're acting pretty strange."

"Not at all." Kari stretched out her neck. She took a bite of her peach, but she was sitting so straight, the juice dripped on her shirt. She dabbed at it. "Just trying some new tactics. For the character awards." She forced a smile.

"Okay, sure." Liza studied her. "But who said you had to bow?"

54

Kari let herself relax a little. "Emily Post."

"Emily Post?" Mandy set her elbows on the table. "Is she that new sixth grader?"

"No." Kari leaned over her plate and took another bite. "It's a long story."

"Besides, no teachers are around." Mandy scanned the cafeteria. "You're in the clear. Relax, Kari."

"Good." Kari slouched over and exhaled. "I'm exhausted."

When lunch was almost over, Liza turned to Kari again. "So, why did you bow, again?"

"Well." Kari took the last bite of her pizza. "Ashley said it would help."

"I haven't won an award either." Liza laughed. "Maybe Ashley is onto something." Liza rested her chin on the table.

"You've won." Kari looked at Mandy. "What did you do?"

"Yeah, maybe you should be coaching us." Liza also turned to Mandy.

"Hmm." Mandy looked up at the ceiling for a moment. "I don't really know. I obeyed the rules in class. I offered to clean up after lunch. Just the normal things."

"I do those things, too." Kari shrugged. "Oh, well. On a happier note, my dance teacher gave me a solo for the recital coming up. I haven't learned it yet, but I'm excited."

"Wow." Liza's eyes got wide. "That is exciting."

"We should come watch." Mandy chomped on the last bit of her sandwich. "You'll do great."

"Thanks." Kari couldn't wait to learn her dance moves. She may not have an award, but this solo was its own kind of prize.

The bell rang and the girls picked up their lunch trash and headed to the garbage bins. As they walked, Liza looked at Kari. "Don't worry about the character awards." She tossed her trash in the bin. "They don't make you better than anyone else."

Just then, Mandy tripped and spilled her trash across the floor. "That's for sure." She started laughing as all three of them hurried to clean up the mess.

The girls walked back to the classroom and the

conversation shifted to the upcoming class project. Ms. Nan had told them she would introduce it after lunch.

Back in the room, Kari walked over to Ms. Nan's desk. "Hello. Good afternoon, Ms. Nan. Mighty fine day, ain't it?" Kari did a dramatic bow. "Thank you, kindly, ma'am."

Ms. Nan removed her glasses and leaned closer. She reached out and felt Kari's forehead. "Kari. Are you ill?"

"No, Ms. Nan." Kari smiled. "Just grateful for another chance to be in your amazing class." Kari did another bow, then a head nod, and walked over to her desk. She leaned over to Liza. "Pretty sure I nailed it."

"I don't think so." Liza shook her head and whispered, "She's going to send you to the office for acting so weird."

Ms. Nan walked to the front of the room. "Hello. Please quiet down." She waited for the mumbling and rustling of bags to settle. "I am excited to introduce a new project for our class! It's a project for all fifth- and sixth-grade students." Ms. Nan held up a stack of paper. "Over the next few weeks, much of the school will be working on a unit called 'Countries of the World.' At the end of the unit, you will present your projects to the class!"

She passed out the papers to every student. "Your assigned country and team members will be on the top of the paper. Along with all the additional info needed for the project."

Kari got her packet and she was thrilled to see that she was paired up with Liza, Mandy, and Max as well as a newer boy named Brian.

And their country was Italy! Kari didn't know anything about Italy. Except that it was the home of pasta and pizza. She was excited to learn more.

Ms. Nan explained that each group would find ways to present what they learned about their country. "In the past students have made recipes, found outfits that represented the culture, or made models of famous monuments. This is your chance to get creative!" She smiled at the class. "Oh! And the standout student may just win a character award!"

There it was again. The character awards. Kari

wanted to be a standout student, but she needed to figure out how.

And then it hit her! She raised her hand.

"Kari?" Ms. Nan pointed in her direction.

Kari stood. "I am *already* a standout student. Because I got a solo in my dance recital. Just something to remember. When you decide who should get the next award." Kari smiled and took her seat.

"Okay. Well. That's not how you win an award. You have to be humble, Kari." Ms. Nan blew a section of hair off her face. She looked disappointed. "It's time for reading, boys and girls. Pull out your books." Ms. Nan shook her head as she walked to her desk.

Kari whispered to Mandy, "Did I say something wrong?"

Mandy shrugged. "You were bragging a little."

"Just be yourself, Kari." Liza sat on Kari's other side. "The best you. That's all."

Kari wanted to disappear. What had she just done? And the whole class had watched her do it.

After school, Kari relayed the story to Ashley as they walked to the bus.

"Well. Ms. Nan probably never had a solo in a dance recital before!" Ashley sounded frustrated. "You are a standout, Kari! I'm glad you told her."

"It was bad timing." Kari clutched the straps of her bag a little tighter. "I felt off all day. The standing tall and bowing and odd phrases."

"Ms. Stritch didn't love my phrases either. She thought I was mocking her British accent." Ashley thought for a moment. "I guess maybe I was. But it's easy to do."

"Are you *sure* this is how we win these awards?" Kari kept her eyes forward.

Ashley waited for a moment and sighed. "Trial and error, my dear sister. Trial and error." Ashley put her arm around Kari. "You've got good character to me."

"Thanks, Ashley. So do you." Kari put her arm around her sister.

"Well, thank you, kindly." Ashley bowed. "Now I only wish Principal Bond would agree."

On the way home, Kari flipped open her journal. There was a lot to write about.

Today was rough. I feel like I'm running out of options. I need to be myself. I know that. So why is it sometimes so hard? I guess, God, I'm asking You for help. Please can You help me be the very best me? The bus is stopping now. Gotta go. Maybe I can convince Mom to make pasta. Mamma Mia!! Talk soon, Kari!

5

Time to Be Queen

ASHLEY

They were having silent time in Ms. Stritch's class. Again.

Ashley squirmed in her seat. Never had Mr. Garrett's class been so quiet. They were supposed to be reading about their "Countries of the World" assignment. Each student had a packet on his or her desk.

Ashley stared out the window.

A small caterpillar inched its way up the glass on the outside. *Lucky you,* Ashley thought. *Someday soon you'll have wings.* Which was more than she could say for herself and her friends. Ms. Stritch had clipped their wings altogether.

One happy highlight was the country she and

Natalie would be working on with Landon, Chris, and Elliot. Their country was England!

Cheerio and all.

Tonight, the group was meeting at Ashley's house. Her mom was making food and they were going to get started on the assignment, gathering information and coming up with ideas for their presentation.

Only first Ashley had to get through the rest of the day. She took a deep breath and the sound rattled through the quiet room.

It seemed Ms. Stritch loved silence. A few times a day she forced the students to stay silent. Not quiet. Silent. Silent was the kind of noise teachers wanted when no whispering was allowed. No giggling. No breathing, if you were Chris. He was always getting in trouble for breathing too loud. During silent time they could work on spelling words, reading, or writing. But they couldn't talk.

Not at all.

Ashley did a very small wave to the caterpillar as it disappeared near the top of the window. Yes, it was very hard for Ashley to do these moments of complete silence. Because when she got really quiet, her imagination got really loud.

And she couldn't actually stop it.

A flutter happened outside the same window. Ashley squinted and it happened again. The fluttering was a bird, sitting on the windowsill. The bird had a small cane and a top hat, and he was smiling straight at Ashley. Then the bird whistled a happy tune.

Ashley smiled at him. Maybe the bird was showing off. *I think I could do better,* Ashley thought. She gave a slight nod to the imaginary bird.

Your turn, Ashley Baxter! the bird seemed to say.

Ashley pursed her lips and let out a beautiful whistle. *Whoohoohoowoohoo!* Just a few notes. High and clear. Ashley thought they rivaled any bird.

Only just then, Ashley realized two things. First, there was no actual bird with a cane and top hat on the windowsill. And second, her whistle had left her imagination and traveled straight out of her mouth. Out loud.

Ashley covered her mouth and gasped. She turned her attention away from the window to the front of the room, where Ms. Stritch stood.

Ms. Stritch crossed her arms and a cross look filled her face. She was double-crosser!

"Miss Baxter!" Her words crushed the silence in the room. "What do you think you're doing?"

Ashley paused. "Whistling, ma'am." No point in lying. Everyone had heard what Ashley did.

"Whistling." Ms. Stritch did not smile.

"Yes, Ms. Stritch." Ashley swallowed fast. "It's very fun. Whistling might not be something people do in London-town. But here in America it's very popular." She drew her lips together again. "You just do this and . . ." Once again, Ashley whistled. She smiled, proud of herself. She felt good teaching her teacher something.

Ms. Stritch took a few steps toward Ashley. "I *know* what whistling is. But it should not be done in class. Ever."

"Oh. But if you tried it, you might see how fun it is. Maybe you would change your mind." Ashley pursed her lips to whistle again. "Like—"

"Enough!" Ms. Stritch cut her off. "Ashley. It is *silent* time."

A wave of quiet laughter popped up all around her.

Ms. Stritch stared at Ashley's classmates. "That goes for all of you. Recess is for fun. The classroom is for *learning*. Please return to your work." The substitute pivoted on her heels and click-clacked her way back to the desk.

Ashley looked over at Elliot, who was still laughing. A sort of silent laugh. They winked at each other, which was nice. Because despite the ominous feeling in the room, she was still able to have a little bit of fun.

Ashley pulled out her spelling sheet. *Ominous.* It worked for Ms. Stritch and this blizzard that was supposed to hit Bloomington.

Ashley raised her hand. But her teacher did not see her. So, Ashley wiggled her hand in the air very fast. Then she held it even higher with her other hand.

Finally, Ms. Stritch looked up. Her glasses had slid to the bottom of her nose, so as she peered at Ashley, she did so over the top of her glasses.

With a huff, Ms. Stritch stood and walked to

Ashley's desk. "Yes, Miss Baxter?" The substitute frowned.

Ashley lowered her hand. "Ms. Stritch." Ashley was careful to whisper. "You can call me Ashley. I don't mind at all."

Ms. Stritch removed her glasses and pinched her nose. This was something Mr. Garrett sometimes did. So, Ashley was glad to see something familiar. "What is your question, Ashley?"

"I was wondering about *ominous*." Ashley tapped the word with her pencil. "Did you pick it because of the upcoming blizzard? Because an enormous blizzard does sound unpleasant and threatening. Especially if it means school is canceled, because I am trying to win a character award, here. And my brother, Luke, is wanting to go on a field trip to see the Harlem Globetrotters. A group of horses, I believe." Ashley took a deep breath. "So even if a snow day is fun once in a while, a blizzard . . . a blizzard, Ms. Stritch, that is . . . ominous."

"Are you finished?" Ms. Stritch pinched her lips together.

Ashley tapped her chin. "Or maybe you picked

ominous because silent time is unpleasant . . . and threatening." Ashley smiled. "Okay, yes. I'm done."

"First," Ms. Stritch whispered, "I don't think a blizzard is coming. And no . . . I didn't pick *ominous* because of silent time. *Ominous* was Mr. Garrett's word. Now please, do your work." And then Ms. Stritch did something she had never done. Not as long as Ashley had known her—which was three days.

She smiled!

"Okay." Ashley gave Ms. Stritch a thumbs-up, keeping her voice low. "Thanks, Ms. Stritch."

For the rest of the hour, Ashley kept her eyes off the window and finished writing out her spelling words. She glanced at the clock a few times. She couldn't wait for recess.

Because she wanted to whistle really bad.

The dinner table was crowded. Just the way Ashley liked it. Not only was her family sitting around it, but Natalie, Landon, Elliot, and Chris were all over, too. They were in the same group for the project. Mom had made a delicious chicken and veggie casserole and they were finishing up the question game.

The question game was one of the Baxter family's favorites.

Tonight, the final question was asked by Erin. "Stargazing or surfing?" Erin grinned at the others. "That's my question."

Ashley raised her hand. "Stargazing for me."

"Yeah." Elliot laughed to himself. "I guess stargazing."

Most everyone said the same thing, but Kari, Dad, and Chris said surfing.

"Great!" Dad stood and began to collect plates. "Let's clean up so you students can start your project."

After dishes, Ashley gathered her friends at the round kitchen table, the spot where she and her siblings usually did homework. When they were all seated, they spread out library books on England, colored pencils and construction paper, and British magazines their teacher had given them.

Ms. Stritch had also given them a packet of facts on England.

They were set for life with supplies.

"Okay." Ashley held up her packet. "Let's start here."

Landon had his packet in front of him. "Makes sense to me." His book was out already.

Ashley nodded his way. "Thank you, good sir." She was practicing her British accent.

Chris wrinkled his nose. "You sound like Ms. Stritch."

"The only downfall of this assignment, yes." Ashley shivered.

"On the plus side, maybe we'll learn why she is . . . the way she is." Elliot's eyes were wide.

"She's not that bad." Natalie waved one hand in the air. "Okay. So . . . England." Natalie held up her packet. "I highlighted some interesting details."

"Me, too." Elliot held up his packet.

"Why don't we all highlight the things we want to talk about." Ashley stared at her packet. "There's a lot here."

"I learned that England was founded in A.D. 927." Landon flipped the page.

"You mean 1927?" Chris looked lost.

"No." Landon chuckled. "A thousand years before that. In A.D. 927."

Natalie nodded. "He's right. And the country's first real king was Edgar the Peaceful. He began ruling as a teenager and was king until he died in 975."

"I love that. Edgar the Peaceful." Ashley exhaled, dreamy-like. "A teenage king. Wow." She looked at the others. "Gives me hope. Because I have big dreams, you know."

Landon smiled at her. "Me, too."

"Well. I have a teenage brother." Natalie tapped her pencil on her packet. "Between us, he can't keep his room clean, so I doubt many of us will run countries when we're in our teens."

Ashley rolled her eyes at Natalie. "One can hope, my friend. One can hope."

"Okay, okay." Natalie laughed. "Who else has an interesting fact?"

"I wrote notes during silent time." Ashley sat back in her chair and flipped through the stapled pages. "There seems to be a castle on every corner and lots of parks and rivers. Oh, and they drink tea and eat crumpets. Sort of like little cakes." She looked up at her friends. "Which Ms. Stritch did not even acknowledge on her first day. Just saying."

"I found some funny village names." Elliot grinned. He read from his paper. "Giggleswick, Nether Wallop, Westward Ho! and Great Snoring."

"Great Snoring?" Ashley tossed her packet on the table. "Those can't be real."

Landon started to laugh, and Chris, too. Pretty soon even Natalie was laughing. "I'd say we should all move to Giggleswick." She could barely get the words out.

"But not to Nether Wallop." This was the hardest Ashley had seen Landon laugh.

"Great Snoring got me!" Natalie made a fake snoring sound and doubled over.

When they finally caught their breath, Chris read from his packet. "Okay. Let's see . . . I like this part. England is famous for several sports, including cricket, rugby, and football. Well, they call it football, but we call it soccer."

Ashley stood and looked over Chris's shoulder.

"I'd check your sources." She peered at his notes. "Because first . . . cricket is a bug, not a sport, Chris. You should know that." She crossed her arms. "And, of course, rugby is a form of carpet cleaning. And football is . . . well, it's football. Someone gave you bad information." She nodded once. "We'll come back to you."

"No, he's right." Natalie nodded as she thumbed through one of her books. "It says so right here." She turned the book around. "Cricket, rugby and football. Which is soccer."

"Yep." Landon nodded. "It's true. Those are the main sports in England."

"Okay, then." Ashley grabbed her head. "My whole mind is blown."

"That's not altogether unusual, Ashley." Natalie turned to Elliot. "What do you have?"

"Ashley mentioned castles." Elliot flipped open his notebook. "England uses a monarch system. They don't vote for kings and queens the way Americans vote for a president. Currently they have Queen Elizabeth the Second. Another long-reigning Monarch of England was Queen Vic-

toria, Queen Elizabeth's great-great-grandmother."
Elliot turned the page. "But everyone loves Queen
Elizabeth the Second."

"So . . . she's a sequel." Ashley did a quiet gasp.
"I wonder if there will be an Ashley Baxter the Second."

"I hope so." Landon winked at her. "You're the
funniest person I know."

Ashley wasn't sure how to take that. She looked
back at Elliot. "What else?"

"I found this." Elliot's eyes lit up. "You know
how I love reading? Well, England is known for its
children's books! Peter Rabbit, Winnie-the-Pooh,
and Paddington Bear. Pretty impressive." Elliot
closed his book. "That's all I got for now."

"Something else." Natalie checked her notes.
"The author of *Peter Pan* was from England."

"That's right!" Ashley jumped to her feet. "J. M.
Barrie. We learned that before the talent show." She
grinned at Chris. "Remember the talent show?" Ashley remembered her accent. "They were Bri-ish!"

"That's great." Natalie tapped her pencil. "We're
off to a good start. Maybe we should find a recipe

to make. Ashley mentioned crumpets. We could do that."

"Also, trying to help out here, but I could be the Queen. Of the group." Ashley shrugged. "Just a thought."

Natalie patted Ashley's shoulder. "Well, like Elliot said, queens aren't picked. They become royalty through family." She studied Ashley. "But maybe you could dress up as the Queen for our presentation?"

"I would accept that, thank you very much." Ashley did a bow. The kind she had taught her siblings. Because that only seemed right if she were going to be Queen of England.

Soon it was time for her friends to leave, and when they were gone, Ashley ran back into the living room and grabbed her sketchbook.

"How did it go?" Brooke was reading on the couch.

"Great. We have England all figured out. Also, we're going to make crumpets and I'm going to be the Queen." Ashley flopped on the floor and opened her sketchbook.

She drew herself on a throne, scepter in her hand, crown on her head. She wore a gigantic cape and a sash. She was the Queen of England, and on the arm of the throne sat a few half-eaten crumpets. Near her one slippered foot was a soccer ball. Because if she were Queen, there would definitely be soccer in the castle. Or football. Either way she was certain.

She was going to be a great Queen.

6

Born to Be a Globetrotter

ASHLEY

Already it was time for another round of character awards, and Ashley wasn't thrilled about the fact. Especially since Mom had canceled any further coaching. As Ashley had told her siblings last night, they were on their own. Each Baxter for himself or herself.

Once again, Ashley sat next to her older sister. This time Kari leaned over before Principal Bond took the podium. "Don't you dare stand up today, Ashley. I mean it."

"I won't." Ashley scanned the room. She was trying to guess who might win the awards today. There was a girl in the front row. She had her hands folded in her lap and she wore an iron-smooth jumper. Two perfect braids ran down her back. She didn't talk to a single friend near her. She looked like a winner. Or maybe it was the boy to Ashley's left. He was doing homework. At an assembly.

He had to be a shoo-in for an award.

Ashley replayed some of the tactics she'd used this week. The bowing and prairie talk and smiling. She had done well on all that. Of course, she could have bowed more. Or less. She wished for a replay button so she could watch again her interactions with Ms. Stritch and the cafeteria workers and the librarian this past week. She looked down the row of classmates and, at the end, sitting off from the class, was Ms. Stritch. She was shushing some kid in another class. Ashley ducked back in line, she didn't want to get shushed at.

She bent over and held her stomach.

"You got a butterfly stomach?" Natalie nudged Ashley. Natalie was sitting behind her today.

"Yes." Ashley didn't look up. Her muffled voice was probably very hard to hear. "Very much so." She was getting used to character awards causing butterflies.

Elliot sat next to Natalie in the row behind Ashley. He leaned forward and took hold of Ashley's shoulder. "It's just an award, Ashley. You don't need it."

She turned around and smiled at that boy. "That is very kind, King Elliot."

He laughed and gave her a thumbs-up. Because who wouldn't want to be King?

Ashley sat up straighter and closed her eyes. Elliot's words stayed with her. *It's just an award.* If only she could think of it that way.

The introductions and announcements came and went, then Principal Bond mentioned something about the predicted blizzard. Finally, it was time for the awards. Ashley held her breath and squeezed Kari's hand. She waited through name after name. But . . . alas . . . Ashley did not win. None of the Baxters did. Another complete and utter failure.

Despite Ashley's very best coaching.

Back in the classroom the other students were busy doing times tables. But not Ashley. She finished early because she really needed time to think. Now that character awards were behind her for another week, all she could think about was that ominous blizzard. What if it trapped them in their house forever?

Ms. Stritch walked around the room, checking work and making sure students stayed on task. She got to Ashley's desk and stopped.

"You're not working?" Ms. Stritch's voice was kinder this time. Even if just a little.

Ashley turned her paper over with a long sigh. "I finished. I'm a quick math girl."

Ms. Stritch looked at Ashley's answer sheet for a moment. She returned it to Ashley's desk. "Good work, Miss Baxter."

Ashley sighed again. "Thanks." Sadness hung on her shoulders like a shawl.

Ms. Stritch started to walk away. But she must have known something was off with Ashley. She turned around and walked back to Ashley's desk. For a moment, Ashley thought she was in trouble. Maybe Ms. Stritch thought she had a bad attitude, or had cheated. Ashley's heart raced, and she sat up a little straighter. Ms. Stritch knelt down to Ashley's eye level.

"Are you okay, Miss Baxter?" the teacher whispered.

Ashley nodded. "Why, yes, ma'am. Mighty kind of you to ask."

Ms. Stritch smiled. A real, true smile. "Okay."

"Actually." Ashley motioned for Ms. Stritch to lean in closer. "That's not true. Can I tell you a secret?"

"Okay." Ms. Stritch seemed to listen a little harder.

"I really wanted to win an award today. And I didn't. Again. So, I'm just sitting here trying to rack my brain thinking why I didn't." Ashley looked at her teacher. "And that's a reasonable thing to rack your brain about, don't you think?"

"I see." Ms. Stritch blinked. "Well. That is not a fun feeling. But awards aren't everything, you know."

"I know." Again Ashley heard kindness in Ms. Stritch's voice. Or something close to it. If her teacher was actually interested, Ashley wasn't going to waste this opportunity. She went on. "And then there's the blizzard . . ."

"Miss Baxter. Indiana gets snow every winter." And just like that the kindness was gone. Ms. Stritch stood. "There is nothing to worry about."

"Yes. But we moved here from Michigan over the summer." Ashley tried to keep the conversation going. "And I've never lived in Indiana through a winter."

"I have. And we will be okay." The substitute started to walk away. "Blizzard or not, we can get our roads clear. Do not fear."

"But . . ." Ashley held out her hand, motioning for her teacher not to leave yet. "If you're wrong, Ms. Stritch, and it does become the world's worst ever blizzard, we might all be stranded here for weeks. Months, even. And all we'd have to eat would be that questionable cafeteria food."

The more Ashley talked about the possibility, the more worried she became.

"Ashley." Ms. Stritch held her finger to her lips. "Please be quiet. Read silently while you wait for the others to finish."

Ashley wanted to shout back that she really did think the blizzard was coming and that Ms. Stritch was wrong. But she didn't want to be rude to her teacher. If she did that, then she'd never win an award. Plus there had been a victory here, whether Ms. Stritch knew it or not.

The substitute had called her Ashley!

After school, Ashley needed to blow off some steam.

Erin and Brooke sat at the table reading and working on homework. *Too boring for a Friday,* Ashley thought. Who could do homework after a week of class time? She stood in the kitchen thinking about her options.

She should take an hour and train for next week's awards. But Ashley didn't even want to think about that. Not now.

Then—out of the blue—Ashley heard a wonderful sound. The distant *shwahp, shwahp, shwahp* of the basketball hitting the cold winter pavement outside. Basketball! Yes! The perfect distraction. She grabbed her coat and hat and a basketball from the garage, and she joined Luke outside.

Luke was always shooting baskets.

"Hey! Can I play, too?"

Her brother grinned at her. "Of course! I was just pretending to be a Harlem Globetrotter!"

Ashley reached the driveway court in time to catch one of Luke's rebounds. She bounced it back to him.

"Thanks!" Luke dribbled the ball a few times and did a perfect layup.

Impressive, Ashley thought. "You could be a pro player, Luke. I really think so. Maybe next year."

Luke laughed. He had one of the best laughs. "Not next year. But maybe when I'm grown up."

Ashley studied him, small and blond and so confident about his basketball skills. "Let's not think about being grown up."

"Okay." He laughed again. Then he dribbled the ball far from the hoop, spun and threw it toward the basket. It came down right through the hoop— without even touching the net.

"You really are good, Luke." Ashley held her ball and watched for a few more minutes. One after another, Luke's shots went straight into the hoop.

Ashley applauded. "When you're in the pros, I'll be at every game!"

"I'd like that." Luke held his ball. "Your turn."

This wasn't Ashley's best sport. That would be drawing, of course. But she liked basketball. A lot. She dribbled in a few small circles, then she ran up close to the basket and fired off a shot. *Swish!* It went right into the net. "Look at that!" She held both hands up in the air. "Looks like I'll be in the pros with you, little brother."

But her next four shots went nowhere near the basket.

"Hmm." Luke watched her as she missed another. "Try this." He came up beside her and pretended to shoot. "Bend your knees. Then as you throw the ball, try to lift it up. And always bend your wrist."

It was a lot to remember, but Ashley made her next shot and the next. "That settles it." She smiled at him. "You're a better coach than me."

Luke laughed again. "You never know. We might win a character award next week!"

He had a point. She dribbled a few times and turned to Luke. "How do you pretend to be a Harlem Trotter?"

"Globetrotter." Luke smiled. "And you have to be tricky." He did a few spins and shot the ball. Even then he made it, right through the hoop. "See? Like that!" He looked straight up at the sky. "It's warm today, can you feel it?"

"It is." A happy dose of joy ran through Ashley. "It's the warmest day of the winter!"

"Yay!" Luke ran around the court a few times. "That means probably no blizzard! Which also means I can still go on my field trip to see the Globetrotters!"

Ashley bounced her basketball a few times. "So these globe-trotters. I'm guessing dancing horses that trot around the globe? Playing basketball?" The whole thing sounded a little unrealistic.

"No." Luke laughed. "No horses, Ashley. We talked about this. The Globetrotters are a team of players who do tricks while they play basketball." Luke dribbled the ball in a circle and fired up a shot. He missed this time, but Ashley was still impressed.

A thought hit her. "Can girls be Globetrotters?"

"Sure." Luke shrugged. "I don't see why not."

"Okay, then. Let's give it a try!" Ashley tapped her foot on the driveway. *What sort of tricks?* she wondered. Then she spotted three patio chairs on the back porch. "Quick!" Ashley dropped her basketball and ran for the furniture. "Help me out."

Within minutes, Ashley and Luke set up the three chairs in a sort of checkerboard pattern just beneath the basketball hoop. And a picnic table somewhere near the free-throw line.

"Here's the plan." Ashley pointed to each item. "Hop onto the table, then leap to one chair, and then the other, and finally the third. As soon as you reach the last chair, shoot the ball!"

Luke studied the patio furniture obstacle course. "I don't know, Ash. It seems kind of dangerous." He squinted.

"Oh, come on, Luke. You said it yourself. You're a Globetrotter. Me, too! I'll go first." Ashley clapped her hands and jumped onto the first chair. "Throw me the ball. Quick!"

"Okay." Luke passed her the ball. "Ready, set, go!"

Ashley dribbled the ball on the ground and

jumped to the next chair. "That's tricky, don't you think?" she yelled. Then she did it again, bouncing the ball on the ground and catching it as she jumped onto the next chair. "I'm doing it! I'm a Globetrotter."

One more set of bounces and Ashley made it to the third chair. But as she went to hop onto the table, she lost her balance.

"I got this!" Ashley wobbled across the top of the picnic table. She bounced her ball, but as she went to grab it—

"Careful!" Luke closed his eyes.

At the same moment, Mom stepped onto the back porch. "Ashley!"

But it was too late. As Ashley tried to catch her basketball, she felt her ankle roll. Then before she could stop herself, she fell hard to the driveway.

"Ugh!" She landed splat, stretched out. A broken Globetrotter.

"Oh, no!" Luke shouted.

Ashley closed her eyes and grabbed her ankle. "Ow." She took a few deep breaths and opened her eyes again.

"Are you okay?" Luke reached her first. Then Mom. They both stood over her.

"I have one question." Ashley winced. She looked at the hoop. "Did I make the shot?"

"You did not." Mom reached down and helped Ashley to her feet. "What in the world were you thinking?"

"I was thinking like a Globetrotter." Ashley limped a bit. "Ouch. My ankle! It's s-s-sore."

"You're putting weight on it." Mom bent down and touched it super-soft. "I don't think it's broken. Let's get you some ice." Mom helped Ashley walk toward the house.

Luke trailed behind. "You got hurt, but you made it." He gave Ashley a pat on the back. "You're an official Globetrotter."

"Well. The Globetrotters are professionals. And they certainly don't use patio furniture." Mom's voice sounded firm.

"True. But I was low on options." Ashley squeezed her eyes shut for a few seconds. Her ankle felt tingly.

Luke ran to the kitchen, where the other kids

were doing homework. "You won't believe what happened!"

Great, Ashley thought. The daily story was about her. Again.

Mom slid the back door open and helped Ashley inside. "Helpful tip, young lady?" Mom gave her a kind look. "Use things for what they're for. Chairs are for sitting. Tables are for food or drinks."

"Or games," Ashley pointed out.

"Yes, okay." Mom smiled. "Or games. But still . . . let's not do that again."

Ashley had more to say. Because Globetrotters had to start somewhere. "But I—"

Mom shook her head. "No buts, Ashley. You're a Baxter. We use things for what they're for. Okay?" She smiled.

"Yes, Mom." With the help of her mother, Ashley stretched out on the couch with a pillow under her hurt foot.

"I'll get some ice." Mom hurried off to the kitchen.

Ashley called after her. "Could you please get

my sketchbook, too?" She took deep breaths.

Luke joined her again. He looked worried. "Does it hurt?"

"Kinda. I can feel my heartbeat in it." Ashley shook her head. "It really was a pretty good trick course."

"Yeah. But Mom's right. We should use things for what they're for." Luke sat on the edge of the sofa. "I'll pray for you, okay?"

"That would help." Ashley took her brother's hand.

"Dear God, my sister Ashley is in trouble again. This time her ankle is hurt." He paused. "Please, will You heal it for her? Thank You. In Jesus's name, amen."

He leaned close and hugged Ashley. "Sorry you're hurt."

"It's all right. Thanks for praying." Ashley smiled at him. "If we could make a safer course, I'd play Globetrotters with you anytime."

Mom returned with the ice and Ashley's sketchbook. "Keep your ankle cold, Ashley." She put the ice over the part of Ashley's foot that was hurting. Mom looked at her. "Stay here. I think you'll feel better in a few hours."

"Where's Kari?" Ashley wiped the sweat off her forehead.

"She's at Max's house. Her group is working on their project tonight." Mom once again headed back for the kitchen. "I'm gonna make dinner."

"If it's okay, I'll go back out and shoot baskets." Luke looked at their mother.

"Yes." She turned around. "It's fine. Just keep your feet on the ground."

Luke grinned. "I will."

Left alone with her sketchbook and pencil, Ashley began to dream about the day. It had been a doozie. The failed character awards and then what still seemed like a smile from Ms. Stritch. And of course, her Globetrotter move, and the ominous possibility of a huge blizzard. Covering all of Bloomington. Even their own house!

Worse . . . what if they were stuck at school when the blizzard exploded over the city?

Finally, Ashley began to draw. She sketched the school building, buried in snow all except the roof.

And on top of the roof, Ms. Stritch, with a sign that read 'HELP!' It was a picture of things yet to come. Only Ashley didn't stop there. Ms. Stritch wasn't alone. Ashley drew herself jumping off tables and chairs to get to the roof. And she had a basket of crumpets for a snack. Ashley to the rescue.

The small sliver of kindness Ashley had seen in Ms. Stritch today gave her hope. And she was determined to make sure that she and this scary substitute became friends.

Even if it meant that they had to be snowed in together.

7

An Italian Education

KARI

Kari had never seen such a feast. Not in all her life.

Mandy, Liza, Brian, Max and Kari were all seated around Max's dinner table. It was the first meeting for their report on Italy. Good thing, because Max was actually from Italy. His family came to the United States four years ago. Kari figured their group would do very well on the project.

Max's mom had gone all out for the occasion. She had served them homemade lasagna and spaghetti and pizza. And now fresh-baked chocolate cannolis.

Kari looked around the table at her friends.

They seemed to be enjoying the food as much as she was. She smiled at Max's mother. "I really do feel like I'm in Italy."

"That was the point!" Max's mother laughed from her spot at the end of the table. "The right food to get you in the right mood for studying about our homeland—Italy!"

"This is the life." Max's father chuckled. "You kids should do a report on Italy every week!"

Everyone laughed. Because Max's dad was funny

and now that it was the end of the meal, they all felt like one big family. Max's father pushed his empty plate back and looked at the group. "Family is very important for Italians."

"My family is very important to me." Kari chimed in. "I guess that makes me a little bit Italian."

"You would fit in great in Italy, Kari!" Max smiled at the group. "You all would."

Kari swallowed a bite of her cannoli. "We need to make all this stuff. The lasagna, these cannolis, that tomato basil cheese stuff . . ."

"Caprese salad," Max reminded Kari.

"Exactly." Kari nodded. "And Max can teach us more words. What was that saying, Max? The word for hello and goodbye?"

"Ciao!" Max waved.

"I always thought chow was food." Brian finished his cannoli as well. "Like . . . this is good chow!"

"It sounds the same, but it's spelled different. C-I-A-O. Ciao!" Max took a sip of water.

"Italians love good food." Max's mom leaned back in her chair.

"Pasta, desserts, coffee. It's part of our culture." Her husband grinned.

Kari wondered about that. For most people, food was just food. But before she could ask, Max's father continued.

"For Italians, food is not just food. A meal is a moment. A time to socialize and relax and celebrate the richness of life. It is an experience. An *esperienza*." Mr. Daniel raised his hand and brought his fingers together. Like he was celebrating, even now.

"*Esperienza* . . ." Kari whispered to herself. She could hardly wait to tell her parents and siblings. She would never see a meal the same way again.

When the meal was over, Kari and her friends gathered back around the smaller kitchen table and emptied their backpacks of items for their presentation.

Liza had brought a poster board. "We can glue facts and photos here."

Brian reached into his backpack. "My mom got this at the store. It's a travel magazine about Italy. We can cut out photos for the poster."

"Love it." Mandy flipped through the pages of her book. "I found this in the library. It has facts about the history of Italy."

"I didn't bring anything." Kari shrugged. "But I'm here to help."

"Kari, you can help me." Max stood. "Let's choose a recipe from tonight's dinner. We can write it down and include it in our presentation."

"Great idea." Kari followed Max into the kitchen, where they went through Mrs. Denise's recipes until they found one that stood out to them.

"Pasta! We can write down the recipe for home-made pasta." Max pulled the recipe card from the box.

"But you buy pasta at the store." Kari thought maybe the chocolate cannolis would be more fun.

Max shook his head. "It's better if you make it at home. Come on." He ran back to the table and Kari followed him. On a piece of blue paper, they wrote down the steps to making pasta. Then they glued it on one side of the poster board.

Suddenly, Kari noticed a photo in one of the open books on Italy. And just like that, a wave of dance came over her. She did a leap, and then a second one.

"What are you doing?" Liza made a funny face.

Kari spun around. "Dancing! That's an Italian thing to do." She pointed to the photo. "See?" She twirled. "Which reminds me, you guys should come to my recital. I have a solo. I don't know the routine yet, but I'm excited to learn."

"Yeah." Mandy pressed her lips together. "You already told us. Twice. In class."

"But they don't know." Kari gestured to the others. "Max and Brian, I have a solo in my recital." Kari spun around again. "You should come watch. When it's time."

"Maybe." Max was thumbing through the magazine on Italy. He didn't look up. "You *are* a good dancer."

"Thanks." Kari swayed, making circles with her arms.

"Kari. Stop." Liza cleared her throat. "We have work to do."

Kari struck a final pose. "There's always time for dancing." She looked around, but her friends didn't seem super-interested. She slouched. "Fine. Back to work." She took a seat next to Max and sighed.

"I thought your moves were pretty cool." Max gave Kari a thumbs-up.

"I appreciate that, Max." Kari smiled at her friend. "I'm excited for the recital."

"You'll be great." Only now Max tapped his pencil on the recipe paper. "Maybe we should get back to the project."

The group spent the rest of the evening finding the best and most interesting information about Italy and piecing together their various parts. When it was time to go, they had a strong list of facts, anecdotes and a great idea of what their presentation poster would look like. And they all agreed that it would be top notch.

Best of all, each of them got a to-go cannoli on their way out the door to meet their parents.

Kari could hardly wait to share hers with her family.

The house was quiet when Kari walked through the door. She carried her cannoli into the living room and sat next to Ashley, who was icing her ankle on the sofa.

Dad was out with Erin at the eye doctor, so Luke and Mom sat nearby at the coffee table playing cards, and Brooke stretched out in a chair across the room, reading. Kari winced as she took in the sight of Ashley's ankle. Then Ashley told her all about her Globetrotter disaster.

"Why did you do it?" Kari stared at Ashley's injured foot. It was puffy and black and blue.

"You know." Ashley thought about it for a moment. "It seemed like a good idea at the time." She managed a painful grin. "I'm sure it won't be the last time I fall off a chair out in the driveway shooting a basketball."

"Excuse me." Mom turned and cast Ashley a look. "It better be the last time."

"That's what I meant." Ashley nodded real quick. "It *will* be the last time I fall off a chair out in the driveway shooting a basketball! Definitely."

Ashley seemed to want to change the subject. She pointed to the small cardboard box in Kari's hands. "Did you bring home a taste of Italy?"

"I did!" Kari opened the container and pulled out the leftover cannoli. "You all have to try this!" Kari tore off pieces of the dessert and passed them out to her family.

The dessert was gone in no time. Ashley gasped. "I wonder if England has cannolis."

Everyone loved the taste and Kari promised to get the recipe from Max so the Baxters could make cannolis sometime soon.

"What else did you learn?" Mom and Luke had finished their game. They were sitting on the floor, their attention on Kari.

"We learned about Italy's monuments." Kari remembered this section from Mandy's book. "The massive Colosseum and the Leaning Tower of Pisa."

Ashley's eyes went wide. "A whole tower devoted to pizza?"

"No, *Pisa*. It's a city in central Italy." Kari leaned her body far to one side. "The tower has been leaning more than eight hundred years." Kari remembered something else. "Italians did invent pizza. In a town called Napoli in the late 1800s."

"Aren't they known for fashion?" By now Brooke

had her book closed, her knees tucked close to her chest.

"That's Paris," Ashley was quick to respond.

"Well . . . technically you're both right." Mom smiled. "Paris does have fashion, but Italy is the birthplace of many fashion designers."

"Right." Kari grabbed her notebook from her backpack and flipped through the pages. "Here it is. Designers like Armani, Versace and Gucci."

"Can we get back to the pizza?" Luke held his stomach. "That cannoli made me hungry."

"Which is why you should finish your dinner, Luke." Mom grinned at him.

Luke shrugged. "Pizza sounds better than vegetables."

Just then they heard the back door open. "We're home!" Dad shouted out. At almost the same time, he and Erin walked into the living room. Only this time Erin looked different.

She had on a pair of brown glasses.

Kari wasn't sure what to say. Apparently the other Baxter kids didn't know either. But Mom did. She stood and walked to Erin. "Well, look at you!" Mom hugged her. "Talk about fashion."

"I know." Ashley whistled. "Super-cute, Erin."

"Really?" Erin bit her lip. "I don't look dorky?"

Kari shook her head. "You look like an Italian superstar."

Dad unzipped his jacket. "We took our time, finding her just the right pair. We were the last ones to leave the shop." Their father grinned. "Anyone for leftovers?"

Mom and Luke followed Dad into the kitchen. Then Erin sat next to Kari and Ashley on the sofa. She fiddled with her glasses. "They're going to take a while to get used to."

"That's true for all bonus items." Ashley lifted her injured foot. "Like the ice bag on my ankle."

Erin giggled a little. Because Ashley had that effect on people.

"Kari's telling us about Italy." Ashley reached for Erin's hand and nodded to Brooke. "Come join us. Four sisters on a sofa. Nothing better than that."

Brooke laughed and dropped her book. Soon, all four Baxter girls were on the couch listening to

Kari talk about Italy and the gladiator contests of the past. When she was done, Ashley told fantastic tales of the Queen and her various castles.

Later that night, Ashley and Kari lay in their beds. Only neither of them was ready to fall asleep yet. Kari opened her journal and began to write:

Hello! Or maybe I should say Ciao! I had the best day, working with my team on our report about Italy! I want to go there one day, walk the streets and see the museums and eat the food. Maybe when I'm grown up...

"What are you writing about?" Ashley whispered.

Kari smiled. "Italy." She looked across the room at her sister.

"I figured." Ashley sat up, propping herself on her elbow. "When we're grown up, we should go. To Italy."

"We aren't growing up, remember?" Kari smiled at the memory of the pact they made to stay young forever. It was still her plan.

"Right." Ashley nodded. "I just mean. When we have some money. We could go there."

"I like that plan." Kari thought for a moment. "We could eat gelato and lasagna. And take a gondola ride."

"And meet cute Italian boys and be fashion stars." Ashley giggled as she flopped back on her bed.

"It's all settled." Kari kept writing. She wanted to capture everything about her time at Max's house. "Until then, we'll dream it."

"Good night, Kari." Ashley's voice was soft and slow, like she was falling asleep. "See you in Italy."

"Arrivederci, Ashley." Kari whispered now, too. She finished writing, shut off her lamp and laid down.

As she drifted to sleep, Kari felt happy for a few reasons. One, she had a new favorite dessert: Cannolis. Two, Max was a good friend. And three, she'd see Ashley soon in Italy. They would meet in their dreams.

And that made falling asleep very, very easy.

8

Where the Best Friends Live

KARI

Monday-night dance class was becoming a highlight of Kari's week.

She loved the smell of the wooden floor and the sound of the buzzing lights overhead. And when the music started, she loved Miss Lizzy's voice as she counted five-six-seven-eight. There was so much to love. Kari's dance outfits and dance shoes and the mirrors that ran along the room.

But most of all, Kari loved the dancing.

They were practicing for the upcoming recital and working on the grand finale, a dance routine to the song called "Ain't No Mountain High Enough." Miss Lizzy was teaching them the steps, and with

107

each passing minute Kari could feel her excitement growing.

Because anytime now Miss Lizzy was going to announce her solo in this big dance number.

"Kari?" Miss Lizzy smiled at her. "I'm ready for you."

Kari could barely breathe. This was her moment! She jumped a few times in place and nodded at her teacher. "I'm ready!"

"Okay, Kari! You will walk up to the center doing a step touch." Miss Lizzy pointed to the spot on the floor and demonstrated the move. After each number that she counted, Miss Lizzy took a step forward and snapped. "One, two, three, four, five, six, seven, eight."

"Like this?" Kari copied Miss Lizzy.

"Perfect." Miss Lizzy nodded. "Then do this . . ." Miss Lizzy did a pas de bourrée. It sounded like "paw-duh-boo-ray." It was a silly name but a cool move. Miss Lizzy did the dance move to the right and then to the left.

"Okay." Kari gave it her best shot. It took a few times, and some corrections, but eventually she got it.

Miss Lizzy took a deep breath. "All right. You will end it with a reach to the left, reach to the right, spin to the right, clap, spin to the left, clap, and hop out with your hands up!" Miss Lizzy demonstrated.

Then Kari did the same thing. "Like this?"

"Exactly. Good!" Miss Lizzy clapped for Kari. "Then slowly bring your hands down. Pivot, and return to your spot." She paused. "Got it?"

Kari walked through the rest of the dance moves. "Yes! Got it!" She nodded and gave the teacher a thumbs-up. "I like it. Thank you." Kari walked back to the others. She could barely feel the floor because . . . her very own solo.

One of her dance friends, Alice, whispered to Kari. "You're so lucky."

"I know." Kari smiled. "Thanks." As soon as the words were out, Kari felt a little flat. She could've said something nicer to her friend.

And now she couldn't take her words back.

"All right, team! From the top." Miss Lizzy played the track. "Five, six, seven, eight!"

Kari felt like a superstar dancing with the group.

And when it came time for her solo, she stood a little taller. Because this moment was about *her*. She didn't have to share it with her siblings or classmates. No one was trying to compete with her. Dance was her own thing.

And it made her feel very special.

Kari's family sat spellbound in the living room, all of them watching her.

"Then"—Kari did the last move of her solo and pivoted—"I finish like this!" She turned and did a bow. "Ta-da!"

Immediately, Ashley was on her feet, clapping. Same with Erin and Brooke and Luke. Her parents joined the standing ovation and Dad gave her a thumbs-up. His voice rang above the applause. "You're going to be just perfect up there, Kari."

"Beautiful job." Mom hugged Kari. "I can't wait to see the whole thing."

"Me, too." Ashley tried her own version of some of the steps. "Maybe you can teach me!"

Luke grinned. "And after my Harlem Globetrotters field trip next week, I'll teach you a few moves that won't hurt your ankle!" He dribbled an invisible ball.

Their dad looked concerned. He took a deep breath. "Actually, Luke, I'm not sure that field trip is going to happen." He looked around the room at the others. "It looks like the Farmer's Almanac was right. A big blizzard is forecast for next week. It's been all over the news." Dad raised his eyebrows. "Could be serious."

"Good!" Brooke did a brief celebration dance. "I love snow days!"

Ashley dropped to the sofa and crossed her arms. "There goes the character awards." She shrugged. "Our time to win was coming. I could feel it."

Erin smiled. "Snow days are more fun than awards."

"She might be right." Kari blew at a wisp of her long hair. "I'm not sure we'll ever win."

Shock came over Ashley's face. Like she couldn't believe what she'd just heard. "People." She stood and faced Kari and Erin. "That is not the winning spirit. The Baxter children will never take home a character award with that attitude."

"You know what I think, Ashley?" Kari stood now. She put her hands on her hips. "I think you care too much about those awards. What does it matter if we win or not?"

"You don't have to be mean." Ashley made an angry face at Kari. "I'm just saying I don't want a snowstorm!"

"Same here." Luke nodded. "I don't want to miss the field trip."

"Why do you care if they call our names at the assembly? What does it matter?" Kari shot a mean look at Ashley. Also she could hear her voice getting louder. Never a good sign. "You're obsessed, Ashley."

"You're right!" Ashley held her head high. "I am upset. I'm upset with you . . . because us Baxter kids are winners, that's why!"

"Not upset. Obsessed." Kari shook her head. "Never mind."

"Whoa, whoa." Dad seemed to suddenly realize what was happening. He held up his hands. "Quiet down. Everyone take a seat."

Kari sat in the nearest chair. Her siblings lined

up on the sofa, and Ashley took the spot farthest away.

"We will not talk to each other like that in this house." Dad looked from Kari to Ashley. Gradually, kindness filled his eyes. "First, Ashley, only God can control the weather."

"Yes." Mom nodded. "Your dad's right about that."

The kids sat, quiet. This had turned into a family meeting, apparently. Or at least it felt like one. Kari's heart was pounding. Because Ashley shouldn't have been so rude.

Dad and Mom stood together, and Dad turned to Luke. "If your trip gets canceled, the Globetrotters will come back another time. It's not the end of the world."

Ashley raised her hand.

Dad seemed caught off guard. He turned to her. "Yes, Ashley?"

"It might be the end of the world. If it snows enough." She did a half bow. "Just saying."

For a moment, Dad only blinked. "I assure you that next week's blizzard will not be the end of the world." He gave her a serious look. "Please. Let me finish, Ashley."

"Very well." She bowed again.

Dad turned to Kari and Erin and Brooke. "I'm glad you're excited about the snowstorm. But, Kari, you need to be kind." He looked at Ashley. "Same with you." He took a long breath. "Whatever happens next week, God will be with us, and we will be with each other. Which means remembering our family rule. What's the rule?"

"Can I say it?" Brooke smiled. She was the shining star in this situation, which made sense. Since she was in middle school. "Always be kind and remember . . . your best friends are the ones who sit around your dinner table each night."

"That's it." Dad smiled. He took Mom's hand. "Honey, why don't you pray and then the kids can get ready for bed."

Mom smiled at him. These two really loved each other, and something about that made Kari feel safe. No matter what kind of storm was coming. Mom waited till everyone was ready. "Dear God, thank You for our family. Thank You that in any sort of trouble, You are with us and You love us. Help us to remember that we must use friendly words and a friendly voice. And help us to care more for each other than we do for ourselves. In Jesus's name, amen."

"Amen." The rest of the room finished the prayer with one voice.

Everyone got started on getting ready for bed, but Kari moved over and sat next to Ashley. "I'm sorry. For using a rude tone." She sighed. "I think that happened at dance class, too. With my friend Alice."

Ashley patted Kari on the shoulder. "I don't know about Alice. But I forgive you." Ashley looked like she might bow again. But instead her smile fell a little at the edges. "I'm sorry, too. Everyone doesn't have to care about character awards as much as I do."

"Thank you. And it's okay. I'm not mad." Then, like a movie in her head, Kari pictured Ashley standing in the middle of the assembly, raising her hand and asking their principal about the rules.

And suddenly everything about that seemed funny. She started to giggle.

"What's funny?" Ashley chuckled a little, too.

"Everything!" Kari was laughing harder now. "You at the assembly, trying to learn the rules of character awards!"

Ashley seemed to see the exact same thing in her head, because her laughter was louder now. So loud the two of them could barely breathe. "I was . . . the only one!"

"You were! You're always so funny, Ashley!" Kari put her arm around her sister and the two bent over, laughing so hard they had tears in their eyes. Kari waited till she could get the words out. "There . . . there should be an award for that! Funniest of all!"

"Yes!" Ashley stood and took a final bow. "And the winner is . . ."

Kari and Ashley left the living room hanging on to each other, still laughing. It was the best feeling in the world.

"Looks like God answered our prayer." Mom

smiled at the sight of Kari and Ashley stumbling into the kitchen.

"Yes!" Kari caught her breath. She hugged their mother. "I'm sorry. For my attitude."

"Me, too." Ashley wiped away a few happy tears. "I can get a little crazy."

"Yes. So I've noticed." Mom laughed now, too. "Just remember, both of you . . . you're Baxters!" Mom put her hands on Kari's shoulders. "That should mean something."

"Yes, Mom." Kari exhaled. "I'm tired enough for bed!"

Later, when they were all upstairs brushing their teeth and getting ready, Kari noticed Brooke and Mom talking in Brooke's room. She slipped in to hear what was going on. Brooke brushed a tear off her cheek, but it wasn't the laughing kind.

"No matter what I do, she's still mean to me." Brooke looked at Kari. "Hi. You can hear this, too."

Mom took Brooke's hand. "I'm sorry."

"I just get embarrassed." Brooke hugged her knees. "I don't know what to do."

Erin and Ashley joined them, all four sisters and their mom sitting on the bed.

"Hold your ground, Brooke." Mom sounded confident this would work. "Those other girls are your friends, too."

Brooke sniffed. "Okay."

"Be friendly. But sit there." Mom smiled. "Eventually the mean girl will see that her ways aren't working."

Kari agreed. She patted Brooke's back. "And you could always bring up something fun."

"Right." Mom nodded. "Change the subject. Tell the other girls an interesting bit of news."

Erin's eyes lit up. "Like how the Globetrotters are coming to town."

"Or the blizzard," Kari chimed in. "Maybe the mean girl is just awkward and doesn't know what to say?"

"She says plenty." Brooke dried her eyes again. "Just not nice things."

For a moment, Erin looked down, then she lifted her face to Brooke's. "Someone at school called me four eyes today."

Kari felt a burst of anger. "Who did that?"

"Some boy." Erin's smile never left. "I guess I knew it would happen."

"He shouldn't have said that." Mom pulled Erin into a hug. "But I love your attitude."

"Thanks. My sisters already told me the truth." Erin struck a pose. "I'm a fashionista."

"That's right." Brooke winked.

Kari loved this, spending time with her mom and sisters and helping each other handle life. Everything about it felt wonderful.

"See? Words are powerful." Mom looked at each of them. "We can use them to be mean . . . or to encourage each other. And encouraging is what Baxters do best."

"So true!" Brooke looked much happier now. "I am thankful for all of you."

"Me, too." Erin pushed her glasses a little higher on her nose.

For a long moment, Mom seemed to take in each of their faces, each of their hearts. "Don't forget . . . meanness only works if you let it work. When someone is mean to you, stay confident, head high. At least on the outside. When you get sad in front of a bully, they think they won."

"True." Brooke looked off. "That happened the first time this girl was mean."

"The truth is, their words don't define who you are." Mom put her arms around the girls. "God has made you strong and kind, smart and beautiful. You are very, very valuable. Hold on to that."

Ashley nodded. "I should be writing this down."

"I'll write it down later." Kari grinned at her sister. "In my journal."

"And I'll draw it. In my sketchbook." Ashley looked happy about the fact.

"One more thing." Mom's voice was warm. "It's okay to feel upset and sad. Some kids have to take those feelings to a teacher or a counselor. But in this family, you can bring those harder emotions right here. Because here you are safe, and we care how each other feels. We can talk about it and pretty soon, everything will be okay!"

"I feel safe here." Erin was still hugging Mom.

Brooke leaned on Mom's other shoulder. "Me, too."

"And me!" Ashley pointed her finger in the air.

"Same." Kari found her way into the hug, cuddling with Mom and her sisters. She took in this special moment with family. She closed her eyes and listened to the sound of Dad and Luke talking about basketball down the hall.

The best people Kari knew were under this roof.

Even after not being her best self today, the night was ending with the happiest thoughts. Because God was with them, and He had given them this beautiful family.

And that was more important than anything in all the world.

9

The Ooey, Gooey, Gluey Disaster

ASHLEY

Ashley's group had more to do on their England project, so after school Tuesday, they all went to Landon Blake's house. The five of them had to figure out the final details for their presentation. Ashley was glad they had the most important detail figured out.

The fact that she would be Queen.

Already they had decided the basics. Each of them would read out loud different facts about England. Also, they would each dress like a famous British historic figure. Mostly because Natalie thought Ashley shouldn't be the only one allowed to wear a costume.

Landon would be the famous William Shakespeare. Chris was going to be Paul McCartney—-representing the famous musical group the Beatles. And Natalie chose Margaret Thatcher, the first female British prime minister.

And finally, after much debate, Elliot decided to be J. R. R. Tolkien, the author who wrote the Lord of the Rings series. Ashley had no idea what that was, but Elliot was a big reader. "I read Lord of the Rings before my dad did," he told them. He seemed proud of the fact. Apparently there was some elf with a bow and arrow in the book. His name was Lego Land or Legos Lost. Something like that.

Ashley was pretty sure Elliot would do just fine in middle school.

So, with their historic figures picked out, they each went to work, coming up with sections of facts to share. Ashley and Natalie would cover politics and history. Chris and Landon would talk about the impact of music and theater in England. And Elliot would talk about literature and food.

Now they had to get it done.

"I'll start with the Queen's crown." Ashley

had brought big sheets of colored cardboard cut into strips. "I thought my crown should be multi-colored. Like Joseph's coat."

Elliot nodded. "Very nice, Ashley."

"Yeah, you'll be a hit." Landon winked at her.

A hit would be nice. Ashley smiled to herself. She took four strips of cardboard . . . red, yellow, blue and purple. Then, one at a time, she covered the strips in glue. "I brought other glue bottles," she announced. "In case any of you want some."

It was an important detail, because Ashley used the first bottle to cover the four strips of cardboard. So much glue it piled up on the paper like thick frosting. "There."

Natalie looked at the glue-covered strips in front of Ashley. "What in the world are you doing? That's way too much glue!"

"And that, my friend, is where you are wrong." Ashley sat up on her knees so she had a better angle on her crown pieces. "I am going to fill these strips of cardboard with jewels. So many jewels, Natalie. You won't believe it."

Every now and then, Ashley spotted the boys

and Natalie look up to see what she was doing. But Ashley was lost in the joy of this job. She sprinkled gold and silver glitter all over the papers. Thick glitter, enough so that half the bottle was gone. "There." She leaned back and studied her work. "That's nice."

Next, Ashley had brought a bag of beads. Well, technically not beads. They were old buttons her mom had collected in a shoebox. But they looked perfect for the Queen. One at a time she began layering buttons over the glitter.

"That's taking forever." Chris shot her a look. "You need to work on your reading part."

This one time, Chris had a point. Ashley studied the flimsy strips of cardboard. It could take a year to cover these things with buttons. "I'm on it, Chris. Have no fear." Ashley grabbed an entire handful of buttons. Then she pressed them into the glittery glue on the first cardboard strip.

Much better, she thought.

So she did the same thing again and again and again, until all four pieces were covered in a most stunning layer of glue, glitter and buttons.

125

Time to put the crown together!

Ashley grinned. "The real Queen is going to want this thing."

Landon stopped working to watch. "That's a lot of glue and buttons."

"Yes, I know that, Landon." Ashley smiled at him. "It takes a lot of glue to be Queen."

The plan was to layer the strips, one to the other, until they formed a full circle, a crown.

Only when Ashley picked up the first strip, the glue, glitter and buttons began sliding down the cardboard. Also, now it didn't feel like cardboard. More like flimsy paper.

Ashley shot Landon a side glance. "Not to worry."

More glue. That's what her crown needed. She grabbed the second bottle of glue and plopped big drops on the top of each button. Just to keep things stable. Then, to hold it all together, she shook more glitter over every inch of the four strips of paper. When that didn't seem like enough, she took off the lid and dumped out piles of glitter. "There. Much better!"

"I'm not sure, Ashley." Landon seemed like he was hiding a laugh. "Be careful."

Natalie was drawing the Big Ben clock in downtown London. It looked professional. "Um . . . no offense, Ashley." Natalie wrinkled her nose. "But that looks . . . pretty messy." Her eyes got big. "It might need a month to dry."

"You are wrong, Natalie." Ashley rolled her eyeballs. "It is dry already. Watch this!"

In a quick rush, Ashley formed the crown. Then she lifted it very fast and smashed it down on her head.

Only instead of the paper standing tall and straight like a crown, it split into the four gluey strips again. Before she could stop them, they slid down the sides of her hair and the front of her face, over her eyes and mouth. Ashley began grabbing at the strips. Only because of the glue, the paper ripped into ooey, gooey, gluey chunks.

Lots of them.

"Help!" Glue and buttons stuck splat to Ashley's face.

All at once, her friends surrounded her, picking

127

at the pieces and pulling buttons and chunks of glue from her hair and face.

"It's drying!" Ashley's mouth felt too gluey to move. "I . . . feel . . . like the Tin Man."

"Wait!" Landon ran out of the room. "Mom! We need help!"

Elliot took a step back. "Ashley, if I had to calculate it, I'd say you have glue on every single piece of your hair."

"Definitely." Natalie was standing in front of Ashley. She shook her head. "I told you."

"You . . . did . . . not . . ." Ashley couldn't talk. The dried glue on her face made it almost impossible to speak.

Landon and his parents ran into the room. "Step back!" His mom's voice was kind and calm. She had a bowl of water and a washcloth. The other kids moved away and stood near Landon.

"I've never seen anything like it." Landon shook his head. His eyes were wide like small pancakes.

Ashley figured she must've looked really bad because none of her friends was laughing. They weren't even smiling.

"It'll be fine." Landon's mother smiled at her. "Accidents happen." One gluey section at a time the nice woman cleaned the buttons out of Ashley's hair.

"Sank ooh." Ashley's gluey face was drying even faster now. She could barely move her mouth. Landon's mom ran the warm cloth over her face next, so she could move her eyes and mouth. "I'm free!"

"Not quite yet!" Landon's mom kept working. It took a while, but finally the buttons and glue were entirely out of Ashley's hair and off her face.

"There you go." Mrs. Blake stepped aside and Ashley peered at the bowl. It was gluey white now and full of buttons. The globby bits of her crown lay in a heap beside it.

"That is trash, I believe." Ashley's voice was quieter now. "Thank you very much."

"You may need a new crown." The concerned look was still all over Elliot's face.

"Yes, my friend." Ashley sighed. "I believe you're right."

Ashley towel-dried her hair and then looked

at her classmates. Like nothing had happened. "Okay, then." A few drops of glue-water dripped on Ashley's arm while she talked. She shook them onto the floor. "What's next?"

For a few seconds the group of them only blinked at her.

Finally, Landon pointed to the kitchen. "Well. It's time to make crumpets."

Ashley smiled at him . . . and he smiled back at her. That boy would always be her friend. Because if he hadn't moved things forward, Natalie and Chris and Elliot would probably stand there staring at her for the next hour. Maybe two.

Ashley followed Landon to the kitchen and the rest of the group joined them.

It turned out crumpets were a biscuit-type thing people ate with coffee. Or maybe it was a coffee cake people ate with breakfast. Either way, Landon's mother helped them bake a tray.

Landon kept his fire extinguisher nearby, just in case. "I'm going to take a fire safety course next summer. I might be a firefighter when I'm older."

"Every queen needs someone to protect her

castle from fire." Ashley nodded. "That can be you, Landon.

"And I might be the Queen, Landon. You can protect my castle from fire, anytime."

"You'll need a lot of help, Ashley." Natalie smiled at her. "I'll help you with glue and glitter."

"You have a point, Natalie." Ashley smiled at her friends. "I accept your offer."

Chris crossed his arms. "What about me?"

"And me?" Elliot took a step closer. "We need castle jobs for the Queen."

"True." Ashley tapped her chin. Then she felt her eyes light up. "Chris, you can pick up trash around the castle."

Chris squinted his eyes for a few seconds until a smile lifted his lips. He nodded. "I could do that. I like it."

Ashley turned to Elliot. "And you can build me a spaceship so I can visit the moon whenever I want."

"Sign me up." Elliot exhaled, long and slow, a small whistle escaping his teeth. "I will also fly the spaceship."

Mrs. Blake set five plates at the table, each with a sliced-open crumpet. She also poured a glass of milk for each of them. "They're ready to eat." She took an extra plate for herself and showed the friends how to butter both sides of the crumpet and cover each piece with strawberry jam. Then she took the spot at the table next to Ashley.

"Ashley?" Landon's mom smiled at her. "Less jam than glue, okay?"

"Definitely." Ashley saluted the woman. "Good tip. Thank you, Mrs. Blake."

The crumpets weren't as good as donuts, but Ashley kept that thought to herself. They were dry and crumbly and Ashley needed a little extra butter and jam to make them taste good. Also lots of milk. When she was Queen, she was going to change the castle food to chocolate chip cookies.

As soon as they were finished eating, Ashley looked at Landon's mother. "So, Mrs. Blake." Ashley swallowed her last bite of crumpet. "Talk to me about this ominous blizzard." Ashley leaned her elbows on the table. "How bad will it get?"

"I think it's good to be ready." Mrs. Blake looked around the table at the kids. "But at this point, people can only make predictions. Sort of like guesses based on the weather patterns."

"My dad says the snow will be over eighteen inches deep." Natalie took a sip of her milk.

"That's right. That's what they're saying." Elliot pushed his glasses up his nose. "And with drifts that's enough snow to pile halfway up a person's front door."

Ashley felt her eyes grow big. "How would we get out of the house?"

"You wouldn't." Landon looked at his mom. "Right?"

"Not for a while." His mom didn't sound too worried. "Eventually snow melts. But it's a good idea to have food stored away. Just in case."

Ashley knew about being prepared. She had learned that lesson when she forgot her shoes for science camp. So what about her family? Did they have enough food stored away? Ashley kept that thought in the back of her mind as they finished their crumpets and milk and moved to the other room to do more work on their project.

As they settled in around the worktable, Ashley felt her hair. It was dry, but there was a crunch to it now. Ashley gave her head a hearty shake, but her hair stayed in place. Like raw spaghetti noodles.

Apparently some of the glue was still mixed in.

When they had most of the work finished, it was time to go home. All of Ashley's friends said their goodbyes and got picked up from Landon's house, and she was the last one to leave. Landon waited with her on the porch.

He exhaled. "For what it's worth, I thought your crown was perfect."

Ashley turned to him. "You did?"

Landon nodded. "It was unique. It looked like a crown you would wear."

A warm feeling filled Ashley's heart. "Why, thank you, Landon. That's my best compliment today."

"Good." Landon leaned forward, his elbows on his knees.

Ashley looked straight ahead.

The sun had gone down and the remaining colors of the sunset stood out behind a line of bare tree branches. Winter had a different kind of beauty. Ashley liked it. She inhaled and closed her eyes. Landon did the same thing. And it made them both laugh a little.

For the rest of the time that they waited on the porch, Ashley and Landon didn't say anything else. But Landon didn't seem bothered by it. And neither was Ashley. A real friendship didn't require you to talk all the time. Sometimes you could just sit together and do something as simple as enjoy the view in front of you. Which is what they did.

And that was good enough for Ashley.

On the way home in the car, Ashley glanced at her mother. "Does my hair look crunchy to you?"

Her mom waited till she was at a stoplight. Then she turned and ran her hand over Ashley's hair. A slight gasp came from her. "It's like straw. What happened?"

"It's sort of a long story." Ashley thought for

a moment. "It was a gluesaster, Mother. Truly, it was."

"A gluesaster?" Her mom's eyes were back on the road.

"Yes." Ashley could think of no better word. "You know . . . a glue disaster. A gluesaster."

Ashley spent the rest of the ride filling her mom in on the ooey gooey gluey details. The story was funnier telling it to her mother, and by the time they arrived back at home, they were both laughing.

On their way into the house, Ashley stopped and looked at her mom. "Of course, I will still need a crown to be the actual Queen." Ashley smiled. "Please."

"Well, to me, Ashley Baxter, you are a queen. Tender and wise and creative. You're kind, and fun. You're the best queen I know." Mom reached out and squeezed Ashley's hand. "We'll find you a crown, for sure."

Ashley squeezed back. "Thanks, Mom. You're a queen, too."

An hour later, before Ashley went upstairs for

bed, she remembered the talk she and her friends had had about the coming blizzard. *Be prepared,* she told herself. If she was going to be Queen of the blizzard, she needed to do something to help her family.

So, Ashley snuck into the pantry and looked around. What would they need if they were stuck in the house for a hundred days? Till the snow melted? She quick grabbed two cans of chicken noodle soup, two cans of chili and one can of something named kidney beans. These would be a great start to being ready. Ashley checked both ways, making sure the coast was clear, then she tiptoed to the coat closet by the front door.

She placed the cans on the floor at the very back, so they were hidden by a whole rack of coats. And while she was in there, Ashley drew a quick picture of a future her. She was standing near a ginormous stack of canned food, with a clipboard in hand, ready to distribute to all the people of the town. She surveyed her drawing and then took another look at the cans, making sure they were hidden. This whole idea was brilliant.

When the blizzard arrived next week, the family would be ready. Ashley would make sure they had enough food saved up. She shut off the closet light and closed the door behind her. She was taking care of her kingdom.

Because that's what a good queen does.

10

World Project from Home

KARI

Kari was now living in Italy. At least in her mind.

She had learned phrases from an Italian language book, and consumed all the materials she could find on the country from her school's library. Plus, she craved cannolis almost every day. Good thing Max had brought some more to school for her and the others to take home.

She was beginning to feel like she was actually from Italy.

A *ragazza italiana*.

It was Wednesday afternoon and Kari sat with her siblings at the table doing homework. She was finishing up a drawing of the map of Italy for her group's poster board. The presentation was in just two days!

"Wow. That looks good." Erin leaned over and studied the map.

"Thanks." Kari sat back and examined her work. "I'm copying the actual map. So, it's not too hard."

"You're lucky. I don't ever have fun projects like that." Across the table, Brooke set her pencil down. She was surrounded by notecards.

"You did the volcano science project. That was fun," Ashley reminded Brooke. Ashley was hard at work drawing the British flag.

"I guess." Brooke sighed. "But anything seems more fun than studying for a biology test." Brooke rested her head on the table. "I'm afraid my brain is going to squish out of my ears."

Luke laughed. "That would be crazy, Brooke."

"Crazy gross." Kari puffed out her cheeks.

Erin closed her math book. "I can help you, Kari. I'm done with my homework."

"Thanks, but that's okay." Kari smiled at her youngest sister. "How about you watch?"

"Okay!" Erin took the chair next to Kari.

"I would pick Mexico." Brooke's muffled voice was barely heard. Her head was still forehead-down on the table.

"What?" Luke looked at Brooke, then at the other siblings.

Brooke sat up. "If I could pick any country, I would choose Mexico. The beaches. The food. The culture. That's where I'd like to be at this moment."

"Oh, okay. This is fun." Luke sat up on his knees and rested his elbows on the table. "I would pick . . . I don't know any countries really. Africa?"

"Africa's a continent." Brooke laughed.

"No, Brooke." Ashley patted Brooke's arm. "I'm pretty sure Luke's right. Africa is a country."

"It's not." Brooke shook her head. "It's a continent. Remember the continent song?"

Kari laughed to herself. She listened to her siblings talk while she focused on finishing her map.

"Yes. Let me sing it." Ashley cleared her throat to prepare for the tune they all learned at their first school back in Michigan. "North America, South America, Asia, and Europe, Alaska, Antarctica, Australia, too. These are the continents, all seven continents, and I will sing them again for you—" Ashley went to sing them again, but Brooke cut her off.

"Alaska?" Brooke shook her head. "Alaska is not a continent."

Ashley furrowed her brow. "Um. It's in the song. So, I'm pretty sure it is."

Kari put her pencil down. She had to say something before Brooke and Ashley ended up in a fight. "Ashley, Brooke is right. It's Africa. You're singing it wrong."

Ashley closed her eyes and sang it once more, very fast, to herself. "North America, South America, Asia, and Europe, Africa, Antarctica, Australia, too." She opened her eyes and gasped. "It *is* Africa."

"Exactly." Brooke smiled.

Ashley turned to Luke. "Sorry, pal. Pick something else."

"I don't know countries." Luke frowned. "Erin? Do you have one?"

"Yep." Erin nodded. "Canada. It's close to Michigan. And I remember people talking about it.

They have maple syrup and mooses there."

"*Mice,*" Ashley corrected her.

Kari laughed. "Mice? Come on, Ash."

"That's what you say when there's more than one moose. *Mice.* Wait, no. *Meece.* Or is it *mooses*? It all sounds weird."

"Meece?" Kari could barely talk, she was laughing so hard.

"It's just *moose*, Ashley." Brooke laughed, too. "The plural for *moose* is . . . *moose*."

Ashley's jaw dropped. "English is so weird!"

Kari slid her Italian book over to Ashley. "Try Italian."

"Someone give me a map," Luke shouted. "Please."

Brooke flipped open one of her books to the back, where there was a world map. "Here."

Luke studied it for a few seconds. "Okay. Got it." He grinned at the girls. "I pick . . . Sweden." Luke tapped the spot on the map with one of his fingers. "Because I like the Swedish chef from the Muppets." Luke did his best impression of the crazy character from the TV show.

143

Kari and her sisters all laughed. Luke was the best entertainer.

"Good pick." Brooke gave Luke a high five.

Ashley continued working on her flag. "And good impression."

"You know." Kari looked around the table. "We could each draw the flag from the country we like best, and present them at dinner. Then it's like our own version of the project." Kari jumped up from her chair, ran to the cupboards in the kitchen, grabbed the box of art supplies and returned to the table.

"Great idea!" Erin rummaged through the box.

Kari turned to Brooke. "Do any of your books have pictures of world flags?"

Brooke dipped down below the table and searched her backpack. She returned with her geography book. "Probably this one?" She turned to the back of the book and, sure enough, there were two full pages of world flags.

"Perfect!" Ashley leaned back. "And I'm almost done with mine. So, I can supervise if anyone needs help."

Kari and her siblings sprang into action, taking

blank boring sheets of paper and turning them into bright and colorful flags of the countries they each picked. Kari's Italian flag was pretty easy because it was just three colors: red, green, and white. Good thing too, because she had dance lessons in a few minutes. She was already in her leotard.

Mom came into the kitchen. "What are we doing here?"

"Making world flags." Luke was busy at work on his Sweden flag.

"Lovely. Make sure you finish your real home-work as well, okay?" Mom turned to Kari. "We're having spaghetti tonight. Because of your project on Italy!"

"Really?" Kari slid out from the chair and walked over to Mom.

"Yes. You're my little Italian girl." Her mother ran her hands through Kari's hair.

Mom grabbed the keys and her purse. "We'll be back before dinner!"

"Five, six, seven, eight!" Miss Lizzy called out over the music.

Kari's dance class was nearly done learning the moves for "Ain't No Mountain High Enough." Kari smiled when it came time to run through the number. Because she knew her solo perfectly.

Each time they went through the entire dance, Miss Lizzy had complimented Kari. So much that Kari wondered when the teacher was going to have the backup dancers take a seat.

She spun around and threw her hands in the air, stepping and clapping with the beat. Kari pictured dancing in Italy. Again, her mind wandered to cannolis and lasagna and—BOOM!

Suddenly Kari ran into Alice. Both girls fell flat to the ground.

"Ow!" Alice cried out as she struggled to stand.

Kari jumped up. "Are you okay?" She helped Alice to her feet.

"Everyone good?" Miss Lizzy hurried over.

Alice nodded. "I'm fine."

"Yes. Sorry. I got distracted." Kari waved off the class. "I'm good. Really."

"That can happen to anyone." Miss Lizzy shot Kari a kind smile. "Let's all take a quick water break."

During the break, Alice walked up to Kari. "You should spin right *then* left." She demonstrated.

"What?" Kari took a few deep breaths. Dancing was very tiring.

Alice stared at her. "You're getting the moves wrong. I could help you?" Alice did the steps again.

Sweet Alice, Kari thought. Trying to help with her solo. Kari smiled and shook her head. "I don't need help. Thank you, Alice."

Alice shrugged and headed for her water bottle on the bench. Kari walked up to Miss Lizzy. "Excuse me?"

"Yes, Kari?"

Kari leaned in close. "I think I've got the solo moves down. I don't think I actually need my backup dancers anymore." Kari motioned to the other girls.

Miss Lizzy looked confused. She bent down to Kari's eye level. "*Backup* dancers?"

"Yes. The other kids. They're good. And I know you had them there because you didn't want me to be nervous. But I don't need them. I can do it all by myself now." Kari smiled. "Because that's what a solo means. By yourself."

"Oh." Miss Lizzy blinked. "No, Kari, your solo is only the bit at the end, while the rest of the group dances with you. This is not a solo *piece*. It's a group piece with a highlighted solo moment."

A trembly feeling hit Kari's stomach. "So . . . so it's not really a solo?"

"Not in that sense." Her teacher was clearly sure about this. "I hope that's okay."

"But . . ." Kari thought about her family and friends. She'd told everyone she was doing a solo in the dance recital. "I really wanted to dance by myself."

A no-nonsense look came over Miss Lizzy's face. "I'm happy to give the solo to Alice if you're unable to do it, Kari."

"No, no." Kari shook her head. "It'll be fine. I'll be fine. Thank you, Miss Lizzy."

"Solos are a responsibility." Miss Lizzy raised her eyebrows. "Don't let me down." She walked to the center of the dance floor and gave instructions on what to do next.

But Kari wasn't listening very well. She didn't feel like a girl from Italy anymore.

She felt like a fake.

Five country flags were now taped to the wall above the dining room table. Kari waited till her family had prayed before breaking the news. Her heart pounded in her chest. "I have something to tell everyone."

Her parents and siblings turned to her. Then as fast as she could she explained the situation.

"That's fine, Kari." Mom passed the spaghetti to Brooke. "The recital is not about you. It's a group effort."

"Yeah, it's still a special part of the dance." Ashley cocked her head to one side. "Plus, maybe you could do an encore solo. After the show is over."

Kari shook her head. "Probably not."

"It's still an honor, Ashley." Brooke smiled. "And your part is still a solo."

"I guess." Kari wondered what her friends would say when they found out. She took a bite of spaghetti. "On another note, your pasta is excellent. Not too al dente."

"What the huh?" Ashley threw her head back. "This pasta has a dent?"

"No. Al dente is when the pasta has a slight crunch to the bite," Kari explained. "I learned it while studying."

"All right. Speaking of studying . . ." Dad looked at the wall as he ate his salad. "Tell me about these wonderful flags."

Ashley talked through a mouth full of garlic bread. "It's our very own Countries of the World project."

Kari nodded. "I did Italy . . . and Ashley did England. Because we're doing group reports on those countries."

Brooke took a drink of water. "So the rest of us picked a country and made that country's flag."

Luke jumped up and ran to his flag. "I did Sweden. Famous for the singing group ABBA, the northern lights and meatballs."

"Nice." Dad pushed his plate back. "Erin? What did you do?"

"Canada." Erin pointed to hers. "Maple syrup and . . . moose."

Dad laughed. "And it's beautiful there, too. Amazing hiking and nature. I've been a few times."

"I did Mexico." Brooke stood and joined Luke. "Because I love enchiladas and beautiful beaches."

"Makes me want to travel." Mom gave them a round of applause. "Well done, everyone."

"It's great to always be learning. Keep that up." Dad turned and looked at Kari. "And you got Italy? My little *ragazza*?"

Kari lit up. She looked at Dad. "You know Italian?"

"Yep. A little." He leaned back. "So, what are you learning?"

"The Leaning Tower of Pisa is a popular location. The tower is actually leaning due to the soft ground under it. The ground couldn't hold up the building so it started leaning."

"I would love to see that." Mom raised her shoulders and grabbed Dad's hand. "A trip to Italy. Doesn't that sound romantic, John?"

"Mhmm." Dad smiled at Mom.

"I'll pass on that trip." Ashley shook her head. "What if that leaning tower falls over? Sounds like a mess."

Kari went on. "Italians are famous for their art. The Baroque period of art started in Italy."

"Now the art is broke?" Ashley tossed her hands and let them fall to her lap. "Definitely not my cup of tea."

Dad grinned and spent a few minutes explaining the difference between broken and Baroque art.

Ashley still looked confused. "My country is England, and the buildings are not leaning. They are castles. And I'm the Queen."

Everyone laughed and the family started talking all at once about the different places they wanted to visit someday.

As everyone cleaned up dinner, Kari stared at the flags on the wall. Sometimes the whole wide world felt only as big as Bloomington and Ann Arbor. The only two places she had ever lived. But learning about the world made her excited about traveling one day. It had given her a look into this big world that they lived in.

Later that night, she sat on the couch and journaled.

Hi there! The world is so much bigger than I used to think. Obviously I want to go to Italy. I want to have pizza under the Leaning Tower of Pisa. I want to stroll down the streets. But I also want to go to Canada and look for moose with Erin. It would be amazing to see the northern lights with Luke. Me and Brooke could spend the day at the beach in Mexico. And Ash and I could have tea with the Queen. Oh . . . And I'd like to spend the morning in France with Mom and Dad. I want to see it all with my family. One day maybe.

Getting Lost with Marlene

ASHLEY

Ashley stared out the classroom window and tapped her pencil on her notebook. Usually she worked great under pressure. No big deal. But not today. Not with their Countries of the World project due tomorrow.

This project had made her change her tune about this whole working under pressure thing.

Changing your tune was kind of like when you start singing one song, say, "Somewhere over the Rainbow," but you realize the chorus is too high. And so midway through the verse you start singing "Swing Low, Sweet Chariot" instead. Because it's lower and much more comfortable.

Ashley stared at her notebook again. Singing

would do her no good now. She looked around the room. Natalie and Chris, Elliot and Landon . . . not one of her friends was smiling. Ashley could almost see steam coming from their ears.

The whole class was working that hard.

Her group talked about their project on England during recess.

Landon didn't like his Shakespeare beard and Elliot was nervous about the crumpet recipe. Chris hadn't done any of his portion of the research, and Natalie was extra annoyed that Ashley got to be Queen. She didn't say that exactly. But what girl wouldn't be jealous? The presentation of England was crumbling before Ashley's eyes. And she wondered if the best idea might be just to scrap the whole thing.

After recess, Ms. Stritch had them put their desks in clusters, so each group could work together on their project. It was their last chance to get it right. The room was filled with lots of talking.

At their table, Natalie put her hands on her waist. "Chris, you should've done this a week ago."

"Well, maybe I had basketball practice." Chris didn't sound very kind.

Ashley put her fingers in her ears. Because at least then she couldn't hear the arguing.

Landon gave his fake beard a tug. It looked uncomfortable. "It'll be okay. Just get it done, Chris." Landon was always moving things forward.

Elliot was drawing a crumpet for his part of the presentation. He took a step back and stared at the object on his poster board. "It doesn't look like a crumpet."

"No." Ashley squinted at the thing. "More like the moon. Or Swiss cheese."

"Great." Elliot dropped to his chair.

Ashley raised her hand. "Hello, friends. I have a thought."

A small laugh came from Natalie. Ashley could always make Natalie laugh.

"Okay." Natalie crossed her arms. "What is it, Ashley?"

"Maybe we should do France." She held both hands out. "Ta-da! That's my suggestion for all this conflict."

Her four friends grew very quiet. Ashley smiled. They must really love the idea and they were just searching for the right words.

"No, Ashley." Natalie crushed the idea. "The presentation is *tomorrow*. We can't just . . . change countries."

Chris crossed his arms. "I'll do my work." He looked at the others. "I'll have it done by tomorrow. You'll see."

"Wait!" Landon's face lit up. "Chris, you should sing." Landon nodded. "No one knows you can sing."

"No." Chris's face turned a shade of Christmas red. "I am not singing."

"But you're good at it." Landon looked confused. "Really, Chris. You should."

Ashley nodded. Slow at first. "Yes. That's a very good idea, Landon." She pointed at Chris. "Your song can go after Elliot's crumpets."

"No." Chris shook his head.

"Yes." Ashley pretended to direct an invisible choir. "Yes. Something from the Beatles." Then she remembered one that her dad sometimes would play on the guitar. She cleared her throat and began to sing. "Black bear hanging out with seven mice." Ashley made a slight face. She was off on the words, but she wasn't sure where.

Either way, close enough.

"Ashley. That's not how it goes." Natalie laughed a little harder. "That's *blackbird*. Not *black bear*."

Ashley shrugged. "Fine." She lifted her chin. "Chris, you can pick a song you know." Ashley looked at Chris. "Come on. Music makes everything better."

"I'll think about it." Chris pushed his hands down a few times, probably trying to get Ashley to finish talking about the song.

"Yes!" Ashley forced Chris into a side hug. He was so going to sing. She could feel it.

Chris resisted the hug. When it was over, he stepped back. "And I *will* finish my pages tonight."

Ashley turned to Elliot. "What about you? How is that crumpet coming along?"

Elliot stared at his drawing. "Now it looks like a chunk of igneous rock." Elliot exhaled hard. He looked at the end of his string.

"Can you say that rock name again, please,

Elliot?" Ashley leaned her head closer, so her ears would pick up the name.

"Igneous rock."

"It needs us rock? What's that mean? 'It needs us rock'?" Ashley had never heard of a rock that needed people. "I might want one of those."

"No, no." Elliot scrunched his face up at Ashley. "Igneous rock. Igneous. It's a type of rock with lots of little holes in it."

"What?" Ashley was lost on this conversation. "Okay, if the rock doesn't need us, what does it need?"

"No, it's igneous, rock that forms when hot lava—" Elliot stopped right there. "Never mind." He took a new piece of paper from the middle of the table. "I'll try again."

Ashley moved herself closer to Elliot. "I'm an artist, Elliot. Let me try."

Elliot seemed more than happy to give up his pencil.

Sure enough, Ashley had no trouble drawing a crumpet. She added a big butter knife, a slab of butter and a smattering of strawberry jam. She used crayons to get the colors right.

Ms. Stritch walked by just then. She peered over Ashley's shoulder. "Very nice. England makes great use of ketchup when they eat eggs and sausage."

Ashley angled her head and stared at her crumpet. "It's a crumpet, Ms. Stritch."

Ms. Stritch turned one way, then another. "Wait . . . okay, yes. I definitely see it now. A very nice crumpet, Ashley."

When their teacher had moved on, Ashley rolled her eyes. "My dad always says art is in the eye of the older. But clearly Ms. Stritch is still not old enough."

School was almost over. Ashley looked at Elliot. "As your Queen, it is my duty to remind you not to forget the fresh crumpets tomorrow. And please get the recipe right. Those last ones were dry as a bone." She smiled. "Also, Elliot, bring enough for the class."

Natalie was gathering up her supplies and putting them away. She raised her hand. "I'll bring the butter and jam."

Chris gave Ashley a thumbs-up. "I've got the plates. I won't let you down."

"And I will have my crown." Ashley looked at the group. "We all have things to do tonight, so let's finish well. When we come back tomorrow, we will be ready! I know it." As the bell rang, Ashley was sure she had inspired her group and built in them the confidence they needed for the project. They would be ready and they would be the best.

Now she only had to find a crown.

"I have concerns about tomorrow." Ashley looked at her mom as the two of them walked into the craft store with Erin and Kari. "Big concerns."

Mom glanced at Ashley. "Well, it's a good thing we're at a craft store. I have saved school projects once or twice before."

The craft store had every kind of item imaginable to make any sort of craft Ashley's mind could come up with. Yarns, beads, wood, clay, fake plants, paints.

Kind of like Disneyland. Except without rides and good food and music and Mickey.

But most of all the craft store had crowns! Ashley and her mom and sisters started on the princess aisle, and in no time Ashley had three crowns to choose from. She picked the one with the most jewels. Which were better than buttons and glitter and glue.

As she placed the crown on her head she felt ready to be the actual Queen. At least for a day. Meaning the Gluesaster wasn't such a disaster, after all! Because it brought her here.

"What's next on our list, girls?" Mom led the way further into the store.

Kari skipped ahead. "Italian stickers, maybe? And some sturdy paper. I need to make signs with Italian sayings on them."

"All of that tonight?" Mom sounded concerned. "Let's hope you're not up too late." Their mother turned to Ashley. "Ash?"

Ashley still walked next to Mom. "Hmmm. Maybe something for the queen outfit. A scepter of some kind. Or a cape."

"That's all you need? Just the crown and a sash?" Mom walked down the main aisle, looking up at the signs overhead.

"Yes, Mother. It's Elliot's crumpets I'm worried about."

Erin giggled. "*Crumpet* is a funny word."

"Yes, but it won't be funny if Elliot gets the recipe wrong." Ashley squeezed her eyes shut for a few seconds. "I hope his mother does the cooking."

They kept walking, but items in the craft store kept catching Ashley's attention. Mom and Kari and Erin were walking ahead of her when Ashley spotted an aisle of bejeweled boxes. They were the most beautiful things she had ever seen. She stepped into the aisle and picked up one that was covered in red rubies and diamonds.

It sparkled and shimmered under the craft store lights. Ashley opened it and the inside was lined with velvet. Then she picked up another. This one was covered in jewels that looked like green scales. These boxes were definitely fit for a queen.

Ashley looked up to tell her mom and sisters. Only she couldn't see them now. She popped her head into the main aisle. "Mom? Kari?" Ashley looked around. They were nowhere. Ashley walked down that aisle at a slow pace, looking each way for her family.

The store was starting to feel very big and gradually it occurred to her.

Ashley was lost.

She heard the voice of a woman not too far away. It sounded like Mom, so Ashley followed it to an aisle of fake flowers. Only it wasn't her mother. The woman had long black hair and four little kids in a shopping cart. "You're not my mother." Ashley squinted at the woman.

"No, dear." The woman smiled. "I am not."

Rapid thoughts began firing at Ashley's mind. Was she going to be stuck here forever? Would she have to sleep on one of these shelves? Perhaps one with cushy felt squares? Had she lost her family forever?

She needed a better view. Maybe she could climb the shelves so she could see across the whole store. She was bound to see her mother and Kari and Erin then. But as she stepped on the first one, she felt it bend. That wouldn't work.

Ashley started to breathe a little harder. Tears

filled her eyes like puddles in a rainstorm.

She closed her eyes and cupped her hands around her mouth. "Hello!" She yelled the word as loud as she could. "Help! I am Ashley Baxter and I am lost in the wilderness here!" Her voice echoed loud along the main aisle.

Nothing.

Okay. She inhaled and shouted once more. "HELP! I am Ashley Baxter and I am LOST!"

Suddenly a panicked-looking older woman in a red vest rushed around the corner. "I'm so sorry." The woman sounded concerned. She was older, like a grandmother. She caught up to Ashley. "Are you really lost?"

"Yes." Ashley folded her arms. "I was walking with my mom and sisters and then I got distracted by your beautiful jewel boxes."

"I see. Those boxes *are* beautiful." The woman seemed to understand.

"Right." Ashley gulped. "But then my family disappeared." She worked to stay calm. But a few tears escaped down her cheeks. "I . . . I really need to find them."

"It's okay. We will." The woman bent down so she could see Ashley better. "They're here somewhere. Why don't you come with me to the front of the store. We'll page your mom."

"Her name isn't Paige. It's Elizabeth." Ashley dried her tears before more could fall, and she followed the employee toward the front of the store.

The woman laughed. "No, no. *Page* is just another name for *call*. We will call her." They arrived at a desk and the woman picked up a microphone. "I'm Marlene."

"Hello, Marlene." Ashley forced a smile.

Marlene took the microphone and spoke right into it. "Will the mother of Ashley Baxter please come to the front desk?" The woman smiled at Ashley. "There. She should be here soon. I'll wait with you."

"Thank you." Ashley looked around. "I think I'll pray, too. Because God can talk even louder than a microphone."

"Yes." Marlene nodded. "That's very true."

Ashley closed her eyes and folded her hands. "Dear God, please . . . please bring my family back.

I promise I won't stop off at any aisles without them ever again."

She opened her eyes just as her mom and Kari and Erin came running up. "There you are!" Mom wrapped her arms around her very tight. Her eyes looked watery. "Thank God!"

"I asked Him to find you," Ashley whispered in her mom's ear. "I'm glad He did."

"Where did you go? I was so worried." Mom took deep breaths.

"I'm sorry. I got distracted." Ashley felt bad about the whole thing. "So much to see in here. Marlene helped me, though." Ashley gave her new friend a thumbs-up.

"Thank you." Mom stood to face Marlene. "You're an angel."

"Happy to help." Marlene winked at Ashley. "Your daughter is one of a kind."

"That's for sure." Mom exhaled. "Okay. Wow. Well . . . we found everything. Including stuff for your scepter and sash, Ashley."

"Yay!" Ashley clapped. She had nearly forgotten about her England project.

On the drive home, Mom told Ashley that she had done a good job by finding an employee and not leaving the store. "Whenever you get lost, stay put and wait for help." Mom glanced at Kari and Erin. "Everyone needs to know that."

Kari nodded. "Yes. Got it."

"Me, too." Erin looked at Ashley. "Glad we found you."

"I was imagining staying there forever." Ashley settled into the front passenger seat. "Best not to think about it."

Back at the house, Ashley snuck two more cans from the pantry into the coat closet. This time she grabbed fruit cocktail and beef stew. She added them to the stash she had started. Another job well done. Before finishing work on her scepter and sash, Ashley drew a quick sketch in her book.

As she drew, she thought back on Marlene. She didn't have to help Ashley, but she had. It was a good reminder to Ashley that God gave you people to help out in a hard situation.

Sometimes, you just had to shout loud enough to find it.

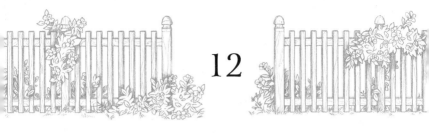

12

Welcome to Italy

KARI

Kari had waited forever for this morning. Her Italy presentation was later today, and her dance recital was tomorrow night. She could hardly wait.

The final piece to her part of the group presentation was a travel passport to some of the popular Italian cities. Each page included specific facts and an assortment of the stickers she had bought last night at the craft store.

Mom said the travel passport was the perfect finishing touch to her project.

Her group had decided to dress up in the colors of the Italian flag: white, red, and green. So, Kari wore white jeans, a green shirt and a red scarf. She did her hair up in a green bandanna and wore red sneakers. She hurried down the stairs and into the kitchen.

"Whoa." Luke was mid-bite of his cereal. "What's that outfit?"

"It's the colors of the Italian flag, Luke," Brooke reminded their younger brother.

"Clever, Kari!"

"Thanks. Pretty much everyone in the fifth and sixth grades is dressing up today." Kari grabbed a glass of water.

"I like it." Erin rinsed her bowl in the sink. "It's fashionable."

"Wait till you see me!" Ashley bounded into the kitchen, wearing her full queen outfit. A crown, a cape, and the scepter and sash. "Ta-da!" Ashley held her scepter in the air and took a bow. "I am officially your Royal Highness."

"Wow." Luke's eyes went wide.

"We get to check out the presentations at the assembly today!" Erin skipped back to the table. "That'll be fun."

"Except they're moving character awards to

Monday." Ashley frowned. "I don't see why we can't have the Countries of the World Fair *and* the character award assembly."

"Because that's missing too much class time." Luke raised his spoon. "It's okay. I'm tired of trying for a character award."

"Perhaps I will win an award for being Queen." Ashley practiced her royal wave. "Hello, dahhling."

Ashley's queen impression was spot-on.

Kari went over her presentation in her mind as they drove to school and when she got to her classroom. Most of the students were dressed up, just like she had expected. She also spotted poster boards and dioramas. The whole class buzzed with excitement.

They had twenty minutes to meet with their groups for final touches before heading to the gym for the presentations. Liza and Mandy were already at Kari's desk waiting for her.

"You look great!" Liza clapped.

"Thanks. You both do, too." Kari gave them hugs. "I love these colors."

Brian walked over to them. "Hey! You all ready?" He had on his Italian colors as well.

"Oh yeah! Gonna be a blast!" Kari scanned the room again. The place smelled great, with all the food from around the world.

Max walked up then. He held two trays of something. "My mom and I stayed up till midnight making cannolis. One tray for our class, one tray for the presentation."

"Yes! That was the plan." Kari gave Max a high five. "Perfect."

Brian pulled out a cardboard pizza box from his backpack. He opened it to show nothing inside. "I just used the box for our facts *about* pizza."

"Well, that was clever of you." Mandy nodded. "I got the list of historic characters." She held up a poster board with names and pictures of famous Italians, including Michelangelo the artist; Luciano Pavarotti, the opera singer; and Sophia Loren, the actress.

Liza opened up a folder. "And here's our historic Italian dates."

"I got the pasta recipe on this card, and I also made a travel passport." Kari flipped through her homemade booklet.

"I love this!" Liza gasped. "We're gonna get an A, guys!"

Mandy nodded. "We really are."

"Well done, Kari." Brian patted her shoulder. "I think we're all set."

Ms. Nan clapped to get everyone quiet. "All right, class! Gather your projects. We are headed to the gym." She looked at her clipboard. "Grades one through four will walk through the gym to check out your projects. A few parents will probably be there, too." She looked around. "Okay? Follow me!"

The gym was even more buzzy than the classroom. The younger kids were already seated and parents and teachers lined the walls. Kari waved to Mom at the back of the room.

Once Kari's group was set up, Mom was the first to stop by. She snapped a couple of photos before approaching. "Ciao." Mom smiled at Kari's group.

"Ciao!" Kari bounced a few times. "Don't you just love it?"

"I do!" Her mom took time looking at every part of the presentation. "I feel like I'm in Italy."

When they had a good number of people in front of them, Kari and her friends exchanged glances and nods. It was time!

"Ciao and welcome to Italy." Kari waved at the crowd.

"Or benvenuto in Italia!" Max chimed in right on cue.

Liza was next. "We're so glad you're here."

"We are going to run you down . . . I mean . . ." Brian shook his head and swallowed.

A few of the little kids laughed. Brian looked at his shoes.

Kari stepped toward him. "You got this, Brian."

Brian took a deep breath and dabbed at the sweat on his forehead. "We're going to give you a *rundown* of this beautiful country." Brian stepped back and smiled at Kari. He mouthed "Thank you."

And with that, the presentation was off and running.

Kids and parents and teachers came and went. Some stopped to listen, others kept walking. And of course, Ms. Nan made her rounds to take notes.

But Mom never left. She stayed there the entire

time, attentive and smiling. She looked so happy and proud. And knowing that she had her mom's support made Kari more confident than ever.

Finally it was Kari's turn. She flipped through her passport. "Milan is the home of fashion and design. Sicily is an island rich with history and boasts one of Europe's highest active volcanoes, Mount Etna." She turned the page again. "Rome is the capital of Italy and home to the Colosseum and the Trevi Fountain. Florence is known for its artwork, and last but not least, Italy has the city of Venice." Kari turned to the last page. "Known as the floating city, this place uses gondolas, or boats, for travel."

"Thanks for visiting Italy." Liza stepped forward. "Be sure to grab a travel sticker from Kari on your way out."

"Arrivederci!" The group shouted in unison, waving as their presentation ended.

Mom walked up to Kari and gave her a hug. "Honey. That was amazing. Just like being there."

Kari exhaled, relieved. "Thanks. It was so fun. Here, take a sticker." She placed one of the

Italian-themed stickers on Mom's shirt.

"I'm so proud of you." Mom shook her head. Then she looked at the other members of the group. "All of you did so well. And those cannolis are amazing. Kari gave us one the other day. I'll have to ask your mom for the recipe, Max."

"That would be the best thing ever!" Kari squealed.

"Okay. I'm going to go find Ashley's group now. But great job. Arrivederci!" Mom waved and walked off.

Liza leaned in close to Kari. "Your mom is nice."

"I know." Kari watched Mom go. "She's the best."

They did the presentation four more times for different groups of people, and by the end of the morning, they were exhausted. But they still had the second tray of cannolis for the classroom. Something to look forward to—one for each student.

"And maybe an extra for me!" Brian grinned.

Since they had a bit of a break, Kari stood and started practicing her dance recital moves. As she did, she said the moves in her head. *Pas de bourrée, reach to the left, reach to the right, spin to the right, clap, spin to the left, clap, hop out with your hands up. Boom!*

"What are you doing?" Liza sounded confused.

Kari kept dancing. "Practicing for my recital tomorrow."

"You have a solo, right?" Liza looked interested. "That's what you said."

Suddenly Kari stopped dancing. She hadn't told her friends about her solo. And how it wasn't really a solo at all. She waited for a moment. "Yes. Yes, I do have a solo."

Mandy smiled. "I told my mom about it. She said we could go."

"Us, too." Liza nodded. "Me and my mom. We wouldn't miss your first big solo dance number, Kari."

The ground felt like it was sinking beneath Kari's feet. "Okay . . . well. Good. My mom will call your moms and tell you where it is."

Mandy gave Kari a high five. "I can't wait. Kari Baxter dancing all by herself on a big stage!"

A cannoli-size knot was forming in Kari's stomach. "Sure. Right." She tried to smile but her lips didn't feel like they were cooperating.

Ms. Nan walked up. "Okay, I've caught bits and pieces of Italy, but I'd like to see the whole presentation."

Kari looked at her classmates. They all took a deep breath. They were ready to do it one final time.

"Good thing we practiced," Liza whispered to the group.

"Ms. Nan . . ." Kari smiled. "Ciao and welcome to Italy."

"Or benvenuto in Italia!" Max came in right on time again.

They ran through the presentation without a flaw. It was their best one of the morning.

But the whole time Kari felt a little sick. Because she wasn't sure what to do about the dance recital. Somehow, she had to tell her friends the truth about the solo. How she wasn't actually dancing alone.

Something she should have told them a long time ago.

13

Crumpets with a Friend

ASHLEY

Ashley hadn't seen Elliot all morning.

As her class entered the gym for the Countries of the World Fair, she kept looking back, hoping to see her friend running to catch up with the rest of them. She needed him to be here. Ashley adjusted her crown and took a deep breath.

Queens remained calm.

She stood taller. And, as she entered the gym, she half expected the crowd to bow. Because, despite the uneasiness about Elliot, Ashley truly felt like the Queen of England. And she was positive she *looked* like the Queen. She had learned a secret to being the perfect Royal Highness.

180

It was all in the walk.

Ashley glided across the floor, barely lifting her feet, and she kept her hands clasped in front of her while she walked. It was just enough movement to look important, but not too much, where her crown was in danger of falling off.

She picked up her pace to catch up with her teacher.

"Cheerio!" Ashley shouted to Ms. Stritch.

Ms. Stritch glanced at Ashley's outfit. "Ms. Baxter. Queens don't shout *cheerio*." Ms. Stritch moved on to help the other students.

Just to herself, Ashley whispered, "Well, maybe they should." She shuffled along the gym floor, her cape trailing behind. Ms. Stritch continued to be a mystery to Ashley. She wasn't sure if she'd ever understand her.

Ashley found her group's table in the back of the room. Chris and Landon were already setting up.

Chris wore a black turtleneck and his hair was styled down over his forehead. Ashley glanced at a photo of the Beatles on the poster board. Chris really did look like one of them! And Landon had a vest over a white shirt. His beard was smaller now and he held a feather pen in his hand.

"Landon." Ashley held on to her crown as she studied his face. "What happened to your beard?"

"My mom thought it would look better as a goatee." He shrugged. "All I know is it doesn't itch as much."

Ashley took a step back. "A goat tea?" She could feel her eyes getting wider. "Because of England, you mean? And how everyone drinks tea? Even the goats?" She looked down the length of presentations. First one way, then the other.

Landon laughed. "You're the funniest girl I know, Ashley."

"Thank you. But where's the goat?" She turned in a full circle. "If we are having goat tea, we should find a goat."

"No, no." Landon was still laughing. "A goatee. It's a smaller beard."

Ashley wasn't sure if she believed him. But Landon had never lied to her before. "I think your mom was right. A goatee is the right sort of beard for this project. If only because the word *tea* is in it."

Landon settled down a little. "All I know is, I'll be glad when I can take it off."

"You can say that again." Natalie walked up to the station. She was busy adjusting her curly gray Margaret Thatcher wig. "Why did we all agree to dress up?"

"It's the real deal." Ashley waved her scepter. "That's why."

"I'm starting to think dressing up was another attempt at a character award. Most hardworking, maybe." Natalie pulled at the pearl necklace around her neck.

"Hey." Ashley bowed. "It never hurts to try." She looked at the gym door. "Where is he? Where is Elliot?"

"I don't know. But he's late." Natalie pulled items for the presentation out of her bag and set them up on their table. A few tea packets and a teacup and a mini–British flag.

Landon didn't look worried. "He'll be here."

Ashley bit her lip, her eyes locked on the door. Elliot was a vital part of their group. If he wasn't here, she wasn't sure they'd have a successful presentation. And they didn't have much time because a small crowd was gathering around their table.

England was a popular country, apparently.

Landon motioned to Ashley, Natalie and Chris. "We should start."

"But . . ." Ashley looked at Landon, and then at the group of people waiting. Ms. Stritch was on her way over with a notebook. Now was not the time to look bad. Ashley knew that they had to start. But she could stall.

"Announce me," Ashley whispered to Chris, jabbing him with her elbow.

From behind his Beatles glasses Chris furrowed his eyebrows. "What?"

She got closer to his ear, forcing a smile for the crowd. "Announce me. The Queen."

"Are you kidding, Ashley?" Chris exhaled,

Ashley's eyes darted at him. "We have to start. But we need to buy time for Elliot. Trust me." She shoved him forward, to address the crowd.

Chris cleared his throat. "Ladies and Gentlemen. Boys and Girls. Presenting . . . Her Royal

Highness, the Queen of England." Chris gestured back to Ashley and led the crowd in applause.

Ashley glided forward, waving her scepter. "Cheerio. I am the Queen. You are welcome to bow if you'd like. I rule this land of England. And I am the best ruler in the land." Ashley looked at the door. Still no sign of Elliot. She continued. "England was founded in the year nine hundred and twenty-seven."

Natalie stepped up next to Ashley and kept the presentation going. "Since its first ruler until now, England has had many amazing leaders. Including me, Prime Minister Margaret Thatcher. And I am going to tell you about England's rich history." Natalie went on with her part of the presentation.

But Ashley stopped listening. She kept her eyes on the door. What if Elliot had slept in? Or perhaps he met an alien and they took a trip to outer space. On the other hand, Elliot could still be at home working on the crumpets. Or maybe he just gave up altogether and decided to abandon the group, skip out on the presentation and go to the zoo.

The zoo was always a good idea.

But those things weren't like Elliot. He was loyal and a team player. If he wasn't there, then he must have had a really great excuse. Ashley was about to look back at the group, who were listening to Natalie talk about Queen Victoria, when she saw him.

Wearing fake eyebrows and a dark suit, Elliot bounded toward their setup. In his hands he held two large containers. He looked sick to his stomach.

"Elliot!" Ashley shouted. Then she covered her mouth and looked at Natalie and the crowd nearby. "Sorry. Carry on." Ashley nodded her head and stepped aside to meet Elliot.

Natalie kept talking to the people gathered around their display.

"I'm *so* sorry," Elliot whispered. "We had to drop my sister off downtown for a field trip and we got stuck in traffic."

"All is well." Ashley tapped her scepter to Elliot's shoulder. "I'm just glad you're here. I thought you ditched us for the zoo."

"The zoo?" Elliot blinked. "No, of course not. This is way too important."

Ashley giggled. "Your eyebrows look like caterpillars."

"I thought they seemed appropriate for J. R. R. Tolkien." Elliot wiggled his fake furry eyebrows a few times. Elliot studied Ashley. "You look regal!"

"Thank you." Ashley bowed. She looked over her shoulder. Natalie seemed to be running out of things to say. Ashley grabbed Elliot's hand and rushed him to the others. "We're right in the middle of this thing. Come on."

Natalie was finishing about Princess Diana and the history of the royals.

"You got the crumpets, Elliot?" Chris whispered.

Elliot nodded. "I do. Some for the class, and some for here. When it's time." He stood there catching his breath.

Natalie cleared her throat. "And now . . ."

Landon stepped forward. "'Ello. I'm William Shakespeare!"

Elliot gave the others a quick thumbs-up. His eyes told them he was glad to be there.

"All the world's a stage and all the men and women are merely players." Landon paced in front of the group. "That's what William Shakespeare thought. England is known for its rich culture and arts scene. Incredible talents onstage, in music, and through the visual arts have all come from England. One of these famous artists is Mr. Shakespeare. He wrote many plays throughout his career. He is believed to be one of the greatest writers of all time. Another famous writer from England is J. R. R. Tolkien." Landon motioned to Elliot.

On cue, Elliot stepped up. "The Lord of the Rings not only introduced people to the world of Mordor but paved the way for some great science fiction stories. And I should know. I love sci-fi."

Elliot held up one of the large containers he had been carrying around. "Moving from arts to food, England has a rich history when it comes to eating." He opened the container and spread the crumpets across a wooden tray. Then he pulled two more containers from his backpack. One with butter, one with jam. "Teatime is common in England. Typically, it involves a cup of hot black tea, a few different types of sandwiches, cookies, and . . ." He motioned to the tray. "Crumpets!"

The crumpets were for anyone who walked by their project booth. But Ashley realized something. They had a problem. So while Elliot talked about the crumpets, Ashley took hold of Natalie's arm. "Oh, no!" she whispered. "What if they aren't good? We didn't get to try them!"

"You're right!" Natalie whispered back.

"We're doomed." Chris covered his face.

Even Landon looked concerned.

One by one each of the adults in the group took a crumpet on a paper plate, covered it with jam and butter and dug in. With each person taking a bite Ashley felt more nervous. If this failed, they would never get a good grade. She adjusted her crown, again.

Then, one by one, the faces of the adults all lit up. They nodded to one another.

For the next few minutes people who passed by marveled at their project and snacked on the crumpets. They had a success on their hands!

"They like them." Ashley took a few steps toward Elliot. "They really do."

"We figured out the recipe. Mom and I." He

189

extended the box to her. "Try it. Don't forget the butter and jam."

Ashley grabbed a crumpet and took a bite. Elliot was right. They had definitely figured it out. This crumpet was spongy and buttery and soft. The butter and jam were a very special extra touch.

"Well done, Elliot." Chris patted him on the back. "You could survive the coming blizzard on these things. Who needs any other food?"

Natalie sighed. "Yes! Success!"

"We did good, guys." Landon put his arms around Elliot on one side and Ashley on the other.

"Yes." Ashley looked at the people enjoying the crumpets. "Yes, we did."

After they'd given their presentation a number of times, Ms. Stritch walked up to the kids, clipboard in hand. She ate a crumpet, and for a moment, Ashley wondered if maybe she was going to spit it out and tell them they had ruined it. Or that the presentation was sloppy. Or how they'd lose points for Elliot being late. But she didn't say any of those things.

She gave them a thumbs-up.

"As a Londoner myself, I know England." And then, Ms. Stritch did something she hadn't done since she replaced their teacher: She smiled. She actually did. Not a half smile or a fake smile. But a real one. Then she said the best words. "I believe your group's project is a real winner."

"Thank you." Landon spoke first. The others looked too stunned.

Ms. Stritch nodded. "Let's pack up. Time to head back to class."

Ashley and her classmates packed up their project.

"Hang on, Ms. Baxter." Ms. Stritch called out. Her voice was sharp as a pin.

With slow feet, Ashley turned around. "Yes?"

"Come here, please." Ms. Stritch waited.

Ashley came closer and removed her crown. "Yes, Ms. Stritch?"

"I wanted to tell you a story. Hearing you talk about England reminded me of my time in boarding school." Ms. Stritch tightened her lips.

"You were in a boring school?" Ashley frowned. She hated hearing that. School should always be interesting.

"No." Ms. Stritch laughed a little. "A *boarding* school. The students lived there. Except for holidays and summer breaks."

Ashley gasped. "You slept at school? Didn't you miss your family? Your siblings?" She thought for a second. "I love my family."

"I didn't have siblings." Ms. Stritch's eyes softened. "And yes, I did miss my parents. But they were very busy."

Ashley hadn't thought about kids living at school. That must be a whole different kind of life. "Did that make you sad? The boarding school?"

"A little. It was very rigorous. Tough classes. Mean teachers. The more you folded your hands and stayed quiet and worked hard, the better off you were at school." She looked like she was remembering those days. "When I became a teacher, that was the only way I knew to educate."

"Boarding school sounds terrible. Kind of how you've treated us." Ashley winced and covered her mouth. "Not to be rude."

"I know. You're right." A sad look came into Ms. Stritch's eyes. "I will admit my style reflects my upbringing. But it's not who I want to be. I'm learning."

"Who do you want to be?" Ashley leaned in closer. This was her best moment with Ms. Stritch.

The teacher smiled again. "I like to have fun. I'm a good leader. I can be a bit wild. I used to be so creative. To be honest . . . I think I am a lot like you, Ashley."

Ashley almost fell over. Ms. Stritch had said they were similar! "Thanks for saying that. You should be yourself more." Ashley stood there for a long moment. "You have a very nice smile, Ms. Stritch."

The teacher looked surprised. "Well, thank *you.*"

"Yes." Ashley felt herself relax. "And maybe just laugh a little when you teach. That's what Mr. Garrett would sometimes do."

"Laugh a little." Ms. Stritch gave a hearty nod. "Good idea."

Ashley lifted her chin. "Stand tall, Ms. Stritch. You can be a queen, too."

"Well then. Cheerio." Ms. Stritch winked. "You're making me a better teacher, Ashley."

Ashley wrapped her arms around Ms. Stritch

and gave her a hug. "You're good for me, too. Sometimes I need a little tough teaching. I think we can both agree on that." Ashley sneezed. And that sneeze knocked the crown right off her head onto the floor.

Before Ashley could do anything about it, Ms. Stritch picked it up and put it back on Ashley's head. "Okay, then. Back to class, Ms. Baxter. There's work to be done." She winked at Ashley and then headed off. "Chris," she yelled. "Stop pulling Landon's goatee."

There was the Ms. Stritch Ashley was used to seeing. Back to business.

Later that night, back at the house, Ashley added three cans of tuna to her growing stash of food in the coat closet. Before she left, she sat on the closet floor and drew a new picture on a fresh page of her sketchbook.

This one showed Ms. Stritch wearing a medal and Ashley's crown. And she had a smile on her face. The new Ms. Stritch. The *real* Ms. Stritch.

Ashley examined her drawing. It was just right. Ashley should have known better than to make an assumption about the teacher. Just because Ms. Stritch was different from Mr. Garrett didn't mean she was bad. Sometimes it took having a little chat to get to know someone. Even a substitute teacher. Oh, and something else:

Maybe even offer them a crumpet.

14

Sharing the Spotlight

KARI

The elephants were getting closer, so Kari didn't dare move.

The cold Indiana breeze stung her face, and on any normal winter afternoon, she'd rub her hands together to keep warm. Or run back into the house.

But not today.

Not when she was worried the elephants might hear her footsteps or see her raise her hand. Today, Kari and Luke and Ashley were on a Saturday safari. Okay, sure, there weren't any actual exotic animals in the backyard.

But the Baxter kids were great at pretending. Especially on a Saturday.

Luke stood frozen next to Kari. "Whoa. Look at that snake!" He pointed to a tree branch a few feet away. "A boa constrictor!"

"And over there." Kari kept her voice low. "Look! A baby elephant."

Luke nodded. "Oh . . . yeah . . . I see it. We should pet it."

Kari saw something poke out from behind the nearest tree. Was it another elephant?

It was not. It was Ashley, sneaking around and making her way closer. Around her neck she wore a pair of binoculars hanging from a string.

Ashley gestured with her hands. "Come on." She kept her voice low. "Let's move in."

Kari shook her head. "Not a chance. Too risky." She could feel her eyes getting wider.

Ashley looked determined. "I'm going." She dropped to the ground on her stomach and began to army-crawl forward. One elbow after the other, her legs dragging behind her.

The elephants looked up.

"If she gets trampled, it's her fault." Kari crossed her arms. "Not mine."

Luke tugged at Kari's shirt. "We should follow her. Better in numbers."

Kari looked at her brother. "Luke. If the elephants get spooked, they could run over us all."

"We need to help Ashley." He took a step into the field toward Ashley. "We'll be quiet as we can."

"No." Kari looked ahead at Ashley, who was still army-crawling her way to the open field. Every so often she stopped and looked through the binoculars. Kari glanced at Luke. "We should hang back and watch. It's better."

"I'm not gonna leave her alone." Luke slid down to the ground and followed Ashley, army-crawling the same way she had.

"Luuuuke!" Kari called after him. But it was no use. He was already well on his way. Kari thought about this for a moment. She didn't want to get the elephants riled up. Only now she was all alone. Which meant she was more vulnerable to wild animals.

Kari released a heavy sigh. Then she got down on the ground. If they were going to get trampled,

198

they might as well be together. Kari crawled forward to where Ashley and Luke had stopped.

They were both quiet, their eyes ahead.

"Oh, no." Ashley put her binoculars up to her face. "A lion."

"What?" Luke stood on his tiptoes. "Let me see. Hurry."

"Okay." Ashley gave the binoculars to Luke. "This isn't good."

"Oh, no. She's right." Luke started to shiver. "Here, Kari. Take these."

Kari held the binoculars up. She scanned the field. Her heart raced so hard she could hear it pounding. Then she saw what her siblings were talking about. The lion crouched nearby. Ten feet, five maybe. Its tail flicked every few seconds.

"I think it's stalking something." Kari gulped. She looked over at Luke and Ashley.

Ashley kept her eyes straight ahead at the lion. "Or someone." She turned to the siblings.

The lion was staring at them now. He started coming their way until finally they couldn't stay another moment.

"Run!" Luke shouted.

All at once they stood and sprinted for the house. Hopping over tree roots and holes, rocks and tree branches. Kari could hear the elephants behind her. She could feel the ground shaking. Luke's shout had definitely spooked them. But Kari didn't want to look back. Not yet. She didn't want to fall behind.

As they reached the porch, she thought she heard the lion's roar. She turned around to see if the lion was right there, inches away. But that's when she heard Mom's voice.

"Kids!" Mom called from the back door. "Come in. We have to get ready for the recital."

For a few seconds, Kari and her siblings stood frozen and freezing, catching their breath. Kari paced with her hands on her head, then she looked back at the field. The animals were gone. The desert was once again their backyard. But for a split second Kari thought that she could still see the flick of the lion's tail out in the tall grass.

"We survived the safari, Mother," Ashley said as the group of Baxter kids walked back into the

house. "Now on to Kari's recital. Where she will be a dance star!"

As she stepped into the house with her siblings, Kari's stomach dropped. What if she messed up? Even though she had tried on the costume, she had a thought that maybe it would be too short. And although she had practiced the dance over and over, to the annoyance of nearly everyone around her, she was scared she'd miss a step.

On top of that, her attitude about the recital solo hadn't been the best. Not the way Kari Baxter usually acted. Not only that, but Liza and Mandy were coming tonight and they still didn't know she didn't have a real solo. She had to figure that out.

Whatever happened, she needed to go into the recital tonight with a kind heart. Thirty minutes later she was in her costume—which still fit. She went to the front door and stretched one way, then the other.

"You ready, honey?" Mom met Kari. The rest of the family was a minute behind her.

"Uh." Kari tried to smile. "I think so."

Mom bent down to Kari's eye level. "What is it?"

"I'm a little nervous. Just want it to be good. I want to do my best. But not get too carried away." Kari looked at the ground. "I haven't been the best sport about this whole solo thing."

"True. You've had some ups and downs." Mom pulled Kari close. "Just have fun tonight. Be you.

In your life, you're gonna be in the spotlight a lot. I believe that."

Kari looked at her mom. "How do you know?"

"Cause you're talented. But as you take the spotlight, just remember that God gave you that stage. Whatever stage it is. Be humble and have a generous heart."

"What does that mean?" Kari slipped her coat on.

Mom thought about this for a second. "It looks like . . . Making other people feel loved and special. When you're in the spotlight, share it with others. You're Kari *Baxter*. Don't just embrace the spotlight for yourself. Use it to make other people smile."

Kari nodded. *Make other people smile.* Something about that sounded even better than a true solo dance number. A happy feeling filled her heart. "I get that, Mom. Thanks."

"We gotta go." Mom squeezed Kari's hand. "I love you, precious daughter of mine."

"Love you, too, Mom." Kari took a deep breath. She was ready. And when she took center stage with the rest of her dance class, maybe she'd even find a way to make someone else smile.

Miss Lizzy taught dance to more than Kari's class. Kari and her dance team would perform in four numbers tonight. But there were three other groups that would also appear on the stage before the evening was through.

The audience was in its seats and the big event was about to begin. Which meant backstage was pure chaos. Miss Lizzy carried a clipboard as she made her way through a sea of kid dancers. "All right, everyone! The recital is about to begin!"

Most of the kids stopped talking. Miss Lizzy waited. "We will stay backstage all night if I don't have your attention."

Kari smiled at Alice and Alice smiled at her. The two of them didn't say a word.

When everyone was quiet, Miss Lizzy continued. "Each group will make its way to the side of the stage."

Kari stretched her neck and did some hops to keep warm. She turned around and saw Alice, who was reviewing the dance moves all by herself.

Kari walked over to her. "Hey, Alice."

Alice smiled again. "Hi. Just practicing. I'm kinda nervous."

Kari remembered what her mom said. *You're Kari Baxter.* She gave Alice what she hoped was a friendly look. "I'm nervous, too. Let's run through it together."

Surprise seemed to come over Alice's face. "Thank you. I'd really like that."

Together they went through all the steps and along the way they gave each other pointers. Working with another dancer had never been so fun.

"Your solo is going to be amazing." Alice took a drink of water from her bottle. "Thanks for the help."

"You're welcome." Kari wasn't going to miss this moment. "Thanks for your help, too."

Miss Lizzy returned and motioned to Kari's dance group. "Places, class! Places for the number!" She clapped and gestured for the dancers to hurry to the stage. "We'll start with 'Ain't No Mountain High Enough.'"

Kari ran lightly to her spot. Even though the lights were off onstage, Kari could see the audience. She saw her family and Liza and Mandy. In the next few minutes they would know the truth. This number was for the whole group . . . not just her. Even so, a rush of excitement and nerves flowed through Kari.

All that mattered now was that she didn't let her group down.

As the music started, the lights came on and the dancers began to move in sync. Kari loved the way it felt dancing onstage. She crouched down while the first group did a series of moves. Then the group she was in stood and repeated the same moves.

Then it was time for her solo.

Kari step-touched her way into the spotlight for her big moment. She locked eyes with Mom, who gave her a thumbs-up. But something didn't feel right. This didn't feel like her moment at all. And she didn't want it to be anymore.

Without thinking twice, Kari did the unthinkable. She spun round and grabbed Alice's hand.

"What are you doing?" Alice whispered through clenched teeth.

Kari laughed. "Sharing the spotlight. Come on. Five-six-seven-eight!" They picked up right as the solo started and neither girl missed a beat. They moved with energy and flair and for Kari, it was way more fun than if she had danced this part by herself.

At the end of the segment, Kari and Alice spun again and joined the rest of the dancers. Then the entire class finished the song with more energy than ever. They all hit their final pose. Usually, Kari would put her hands in the air and do jazz hands. But this time, Kari decided to pose back to back with Alice.

It only seemed right.

The audience leapt to its feet, and Kari was overwhelmed with the sound of thunderous applause. The class took a bow and hurried offstage.

As they left the stage, Alice turned to Kari. "Thanks." She gave Kari a quick hug. "You didn't have to do that."

Kari was breathless. "But it was way more fun."

When they had finished the entire recital, Miss Lizzy pushed her way through the crowded back-stage area to Kari. "That was amazing. And I loved how you added in Alice. Very nice."

"The moment felt more like a duo. Not a solo. And thanks for letting me have that part." Kari hugged her dance teacher. "You could have picked any other dancer. Everyone is so talented."

"Well, now. That is the Kari Baxter I know. And you're welcome." Miss Lizzy patted Kari's back. "Go to the lobby. Your family wants to say hi!"

Kari followed the other dancers to the lobby, and as she reached her family, Kari's parents and siblings cheered again. Dad presented her with roses.

"The princess." Dad kissed Kari's forehead. "You did so well, sweetheart."

"Thanks, Dad." Kari smelled the flowers. "These are beautiful."

Just then Mandy and Liza and their mothers walked up. "Well done, girl." Liza high-fived Kari.

"Yes, good job!" Mandy looked confused. "But what happened to your solo?"

Kari shrugged. "It was never really a solo. I had it wrong . . . and then I didn't know how to tell you."

Peace filled Kari and every word felt better than the last. There was nothing like honesty to make a girl feel amazing.

Liza put her hands on her hips. "You could tell us anything, Kari. We don't care if you have a solo or not. We were going to come watch you dance, either way!"

Kari gave the girls a group hug. "It's like my mom always says. Just be yourself!"

When Kari's friends and their moms left, Kari and her family walked to the car. Mom walked next to Kari. "Beautiful job, honey."

"I took your advice." Kari looked into her mother's eyes as they reached the van.

"I noticed that." Mom grinned. "I especially liked the impromptu duet."

"Use our spotlight to bless others." Kari shrugged. "Someone special taught me that."

"I'll remember tonight forever." Her mother put her arm around Kari's shoulders.

On the way home, Kari's siblings all talked at once, remembering some of the moves from the night. This, right here, was the most fun part of dance. Not being on a stage by herself.

But remembering that dance was supposed to be a good time—for everyone.

Before she fell asleep, Kari pulled out her journal. For a long time, she looked out the window, gathering her thoughts. Then she began to write:

Hello there! It's me. Tonight was my dance recital only instead of thinking about my routine, right now I'm thinking about all the things I learned. Things that have nothing to do with dance. When God gives me a stage in the future, I'm always going to bring other people into the spotlight with me. Because in dance and in life, the most important thing is caring for others. I'm going to hold on to that truth as long as I live.
Sweet dreams!
Kari

15

The Most Deserving Person

ASHLEY

Snow was on Ashley's brain as she fell asleep. Because tomorrow was the day of the big blizzard. They'd probably be buried in snowdrifts before lunchtime.

So when Ashley opened her eyes that morning she shot straight out of bed. She couldn't get to her window fast enough. She flung open the curtains expecting to see a blur of snowy white. But instead, a stream of light filled the whole room.

"Ashley!" Kari's voice sounded groggy. "Too bright."

Ashley's eyes adjusted. Sunlight was not a good sign of snow. Sure enough, the front yard was as green as it had been yesterday.

"Anything?" Kari shuffled to the window.

"Nope." Ashley sighed. "Maybe this year, that silly farmer's almond hat had bad information." She plopped back down on her bed.

"Well, that's too bad." Kari yawned as she walked out of the room.

Ashley turned her attention to the window. "Come on, snow," she whispered. "Don't be shy."

She waited for a few seconds. Nothing. So she walked back to the window and stared at the blue sky. Still nothing. "Fine." She said the word just to herself. She hadn't wanted the blizzard in the first place. Kari had talked her into looking forward to it.

With a heavy heart, Ashley dressed for school but not without keeping one eyeball on the window. Even a single snowflake could mean the blizzard was still coming.

On the drive to school, it was the same. Ashley kept her forehead pressed against the cold glass window, looking straight up. Her attention locked on the sky.

"Ashley. You might hurt your eyes doing that,"

Dad called out from the driver's seat.

"It's okay. If that happens I can always borrow Erin's glasses." Ashley laughed at her clever joke.

"Hey." Erin didn't smile. "I don't need them cause I hurt my eyes staring straight up at the sky for hours. I was just born with bad eyes."

"True." Ashley patted Erin's knee. "I'm sorry about that comment. Plus you do look very beautiful in your glasses, Erin."

Her sister's smile found its way back to her face. "Thank you, Ashley."

"Dad." Ashley pressed her hand against the window. "I have to stare at the sky cause I'm waiting for the snowstorm." She looked at her father in the rearview mirror. "It'll hit us any moment."

"No! We don't want it to snow. I have my field trip," Luke shouted from the backseat.

Ashley finally glanced away from the window. "Luke, come on. A blizzard is way more fun than a field trip."

"Maybe to you. But I don't want to miss it." Luke looked out the window. "Stay up there, snow. Please!"

"Dad! Luke's telling the snow to stay in the clouds." Ashley wanted her father to figure this out.

"Look. Luke can't control the weather." Their dad laughed a soft laugh. "Only God can do that. Now," he continued, "the weatherman called for snow today. But it might hit tomorrow. That happens because people cannot control the clouds." Dad made eye contact with Ashley again. "We will just have to wait and see."

As they pulled up to school, Ashley thought about her father's answer. How would she get anything done today, waiting for that first snowflake?

The classroom wasn't any better. Everyone was wondering when the blizzard was going to hit. Ashley found herself gathered around the window, along with most of the class.

The bell rang and Ms. Stritch joined them. "All right. We must get to work. Math awaits."

"I like to say adventure awaits." Ashley turned to Ms. Stritch. "Besides, we're all waiting for the snow. How can we possibly think about math at a time like this?" Ashley was certain that with the ice broken from last week's chat, Ms. Stritch would be easily swayed.

She was wrong.

"Ashley." Ms. Stritch pressed her lips together. "Don't push it."

"Yes, ma'am." Ashley shrugged. "And on the bright side, you *did* call me Ashley." She looked at their teacher. "Speaking of the bright side, if we get snow, that means no homework. Right?"

"Wrong. I have a spelling packet and a math packet ready on my desk should the snow arrive." Ms. Stritch removed her glasses from the top of her head and placed them on her nose.

"Nice." Ashley forgot to smile. "You're very prepared. That's good." Of course, Ms. Stritch had a plan for the snow. Having fun in the classroom would have to take some practice, apparently.

Ms. Stritch clapped her hands. "You heard me, students. To your seats."

As they found their places at their desks, Chris raised his hand. "Ms. Stritch!" he shouted from the back.

Ms. Stritch pointed at him. "Yes, Christopher?"

"My dad said the blizzard is on its way." Chris sounded nervous. A rare thing for that boy. He kept talking. "He also said we need to be prepared for the worst of it."

Ashley looked at Ms. Stritch. "It's all right. I've got this one." Before their teacher could respond, Ashley stood and faced Chris. "Well, Chris. You see, Ms. Stritch can't answer you because she does not control the weather." Ashley looked around the room. "Shocking, I know. But actually, only God controls the weather." She did a slight bow. "That is all."

Then she sat back down and saluted Ms. Stritch.

Her teacher looked frozen. Like she was standing in her own personal snowbank. After a few seconds she smoothed the wrinkles from her dress. "Yes, well. I can take it from here. Thank you, Ashley."

Ashley nodded. "Not a problem."

"I will need you to take your seat, Ms. Baxter." Ms. Stritch raised her eyebrows halfway up her forehead.

The whole Ms. Baxter thing wasn't a good sign.

216

So Ashley sat down quick and zipped her mouth. At least for now.

"Enough about the snow, class." Ms. Stritch seemed like she was trying to find control here. "We need to get to the gym for the character award ceremony. Everyone line up at the door please." Ms. Stritch went to her desk to grab a binder.

Ashley gulped.

The character awards. She forgot they had been moved to today. And even though she knew that the likelihood of her winning by now was very small, she wondered if maybe today was the day. Maybe she would finally win and then snow would fall for a month, and it really would be the best day ever.

Just like in Ashley's classroom, the gym was full of conversations about the snow. That's all anyone wanted to talk about.

"Hello, students and teachers." Principal Bond stepped up to the mic. "We know there is *snow* much excitement about the possibility of a blizzard."

A few kids laughed at his joke. Most of them just blinked.

The principal went on. "This could be the biggest storm Bloomington has seen in years. If predictions are correct, we could be out of school all the rest of this week."

The entire gym erupted in cheers and applause.

Principal Bond looked like he wasn't sure how to take all that clapping. Especially about missing school. But he decided to move on. "Now." He smiled. "It is my honor to announce another round of character awards."

From the place where she sat on the floor, Ashley felt herself slump a little. Like she was melting into the gymnasium wood floor. This was probably not the day she would win. None of the Baxters would win. No matter how much practice and effort they put into this thing.

Principal Bond rambled through the first names, and Ashley gave a polite clap for each of them. Marsha Hall, who had never missed a day. Rudy Jacobs, who helped wipe down the tables at lunch. And Savannah Brown, who stayed after school three days in a row and organized the books in the library.

Ashley gave her forehead a soft smack. Why hadn't she thought of those things?

Then Principal Bond grabbed the last certificate. "Finally. The last character award of the week. This one is for most sincere, and it goes to . . . Erin Baxter!"

Ashley was instantly on her feet. "Yes! That's my sister! Yes, she is!" Ashley raised her hands and danced in three full circles before she looked around. The place was very quiet. Most of the other students from every class were watching her.

Erin hadn't even stood up to accept her award.

Ashley felt her face get hot and her feet seemed a little dizzy. She gave a very small wave to her sister. "Way to go, Erin BAXTER!" Ashley yelled across the gym. Then she waved off the crowd and sat down again.

Finally, Erin stood and skipped to the front of the gym for her award. That's when the rest of the school clapped. In a normal sort of way. Ashley joined them. There could never be enough clapping for Erin!

Landon, who was sitting behind Ashley, leaned

forward. "Very supportive, Ashley. I liked it."

Ashley felt the heat in her face cool a little. She whispered her answer. "I try, Landon. I definitely try." She glanced at Principal Bond, to make sure he didn't see her talking. "I do think it's all the training."

"What?" Landon didn't seem to understand.

Ashley shook her head. "Never mind." Because maybe most kids didn't practice for character awards. "It's a highlight of my life. I can tell you that."

Erin had her award now and she was walking back to her class on the other side of the bleachers. Through every step Ashley felt more proud.

Because it was true, what she had told Landon. For Ashley, watching Erin win today was better than getting an award herself. Erin had struggled through getting glasses. And then being the youngest girl, Erin sometimes felt left out. But she *was* special, and kind, and respectful. And definitely very sincere.

Then a very important fact hit Ashley smack in her face.

If Erin deserved her character award, then maybe the other winners had deserved theirs, too. Marsha Hall and Rudy Jacobs and every other kid who won today and all the weeks before. She wasn't sad anymore about not getting a character award.

Ashley was just happy to be at a school with so much character.

And suddenly, that was a feeling even better than winning.

By recess time, clouds covered the sun and Ashley couldn't feel her face, which meant the snow was on its way. That afternoon no one really played on the playground. It was too cold. A few kids shot hoops. And some were on the swings. But Ashley and her friends stood huddled in a close circle to keep warm. All of them looking up.

"Gee, it sh-sh-sure feels like it's gonna be a big blizzard." Elliot's teeth were chattering.

Chris stood there with his arms crossed tight around his body and his shoulders high near his ears. He looked miserable. "Probably. I mean, if it's gonna be this cold, it has to snow."

"Where's your jacket?" Ashley squinted her eyes.

"The sun was shining this morning." Chris rubbed his arms. "I didn't bring one."

"It is winter, Chris." Landon started to take his coat off. "You wanna use mine for a while?"

"No." Chris crossed his arms more tightly. "I'm fine. Recess is almost over."

Natalie bounced up and down, trying to stay warm. "Can't we just go inside?"

"The clouds are gathering." Elliot peered at the sky. "Nimbostratus clouds."

"Nimble—what?" Ashley blinked a few times. Elliot knew so many things. He was a helpful guy to have around.

"Nimbostratus." Elliot laughed. "The dark, thick, gray clouds up there. The ones moving in now. They are definitely indicators of a wintry mix." Elliot shoved his hands in his coat pockets and took a deep inhale. "Snow is on its way."

"Yay!" Ashley clapped her hands and spun around. "That is great news, Elliot. Hey, maybe you should be a weatherman."

"Maybe I will." Elliot puffed his chest up and stood a little taller.

"What will you all do? When it snows? I can't wait to sled." Landon's question helped everyone forget the cold.

"Definitely sledding. And building a snowman." Elliot chimed in. "I also like hot cocoa with tiny marshmallows."

"My mom makes great hot chocolate. And we might make a fort out back." Ashley closed her eyes and pictured building a fort from the back door to the rock near the stream. That would really be something.

"I will be mostly reading." Natalie held her scarf close to her neck. "I am not a fan of this *weather*."

"But, Natalie . . . winter is the most beautiful thing in the world." Ashley was shocked. But then again, Natalie was her unlikely friend. No surprise that they saw snow from different sides of the mirror. Ashley put her hand on her friend's shoulder. "Don't you think it's the most beautiful thing in the world, Natalie?"

"Yes. I do. But only from the inside." Natalie smiled. "We can agree on that."

"I like all of it." Chris wasn't standing as stiff now. "Snow days are the best."

Recess ended and they were headed back inside when the best thing happened. Small, baby snowflakes began to fall. Ashley held her hands straight out. "It's here!" she shouted. "The blizzard is here, ladies and gentlemen!"

Natalie and Chris and Elliot and Landon looked at Ashley and then at the snow, and back to Ashley again. "I'm afraid to tell you." Elliot spoke with a soft voice, like he didn't want to burst Ashley's bubble. "This"—he pointed to the snowflakes—"is not a blizzard, Ashley. Not yet."

"It's a baby blizzard. A newborn." Ashley twirled and kicked a few kicks. Then she did eight jumping jacks so she'd be ready to run for the school door if the blizzard got any worse.

And it did get worse!

By the time the five friends were halfway to their classroom door the snowflakes were larger and shaped like beautiful art pieces. "Did you know"—Ashley looked around the group—"no two snowflakes are exactly alike?"

"I did know." Landon rubbed his hands together. "God makes each one unique."

"Talk about an Artist!" Ashley smiled. "And guess what?" She held her hands out to her sides. "He makes each of us unique, too!"

The group hurried into the classroom, snow-flakes sticking to their hair and shoulders. It was the happiest sight, and now the snow was pouring down. But as Ashley walked to her seat, a nervous feeling landed on her. They still had an hour before it was time to go home, and she wasn't ready to be stuck forever here at school.

No offense to her friends and Ms. Stritch.

Ashley did a U-turn and walked straight to Ms. Stritch's desk. She needed to tell their substitute teacher to call off school so they could get home. When she was a few feet away, Ashley raised her hand.

But before Ms. Stritch could call on her, Principal Bond's voice came over the loudspeaker. "Boys and Girls, school is canceled tomorrow and there's a good chance it'll be canceled all week."

Ashley danced her happiest dance, and around the classroom, the other students did the same thing. But Ashley still had concerns. She raised her hand again.

"When you're up at my desk"—Ms. Stritch looked half patient—"you don't need to raise your hand, Ashley."

She let her hand drop to her side. "Very well." Ashley pointed out the classroom window. "It's snowing very hard, Ms. Stritch. I'm sure you remember this sort of snow from England."

"Yes, Ashley." A smile almost broke out on Ms. Stritch's face. "Yes, I do."

"Right, then please will you call an end to this school day? Before the blizzard buries us here forever?"

"Ashley." Ms. Stitch stared at her. "The blizzard will not bury us here in the next fifty minutes. Which is how long we have till the final bell today. Now, please, return to your desk."

For a long few seconds, Ashley stared out the

window. "That is very fast snow, Ms. Stritch. You might want to take a look."

"Go to your desk." Ms. Stritch didn't say *please* this time. She also didn't look out the window. Which meant Ashley was out of options.

When she was back at her desk, she noticed Natalie slumped down in her seat. "What's wrong, my friend?" Ashley studied her friend's face. "Snow got you down?"

"Not really." Natalie stared at her desk. "It's just . . . my mom said we needed to go shopping for food, and now . . . what if we can't get out and we starve to death?"

Ashley nodded, thoughtful. "That's a real possibility, Natalie." An idea hit Ashley. "Hey! Maybe you and your family should spend the blizzard with my family. We have lots of food!" Ashley dropped her voice to a whisper. She looked one way, then the other. "Can I let you in on a secret?"

A ray of hope lit up Natalie's face. "Okay."

"Here's the secret." Ashley could feel the sparkle in her eyes. "I've been storing away food for the last few weeks. A few cans at a time. So my family has enough to eat while we're stuck inside."

"You have?" Natalie blinked a few times. "Where did you get it?"

"From our kitchen! Lots of food." She was still whispering. "I'm storing it in our coat closet."

"Yes, but . . ." Natalie made a baffled face. "It's not more food. It's the same food in a different spot."

"Every little bit helps." Ashley tried not to look too much like a superhero. "Just doing my part."

"You didn't get *extra* food, though . . . you just . . ." A laugh slipped through Natalie's lips. "Never mind, Ashley. I'm glad you're prepared."

"Yes, me, too, Natalie." Ashley nodded.

Ms. Stritch stood at the front of the room now, a stack of packets in her arms. "Should we be snowed in for the next week, you will have plenty to keep you busy. Your packets have spelling and math work, and I encourage you to read an hour a day."

Ashley frowned. She stared at her teacher and made her eyes wide. Then she mouthed the words *No math.* She waved both arms high in the air and this time she spoke the words out loud. "No math! Please, no math!"

Ms. Stritch caught Ashley's eyes and she seemed to relax a little. "Okay. On second thought, forget the math in your packet. Just work on your spelling words." She winked at Ashley.

As she passed Ashley's desk, Ms. Stritch bent down. "You're welcome."

"Thank you. That's super kind. I'd rather spend time in the snow than on my times tables." Ashley stuffed the packet in her bag.

"I don't blame you." Ms. Stritch put her hand on Ashley's back. "You're a gem, Ashley Baxter. I hope you have a fabulous snow adventure."

"You're a gem, too." Ashley smiled at her teacher.

The bell rang and the kids sprinted to the door. Already snow covered the ground. Ashley could hardly wait to get home and start their snow adventure.

Ashley met her siblings at the pickup lane in front of the school. Mom would be here any minute. Ashley took the spot on the bench next to Erin.

In her hand, Erin held her award. Her eyes were

locked on it. "I can't believe I won."

"Out of all the people in our character class coaching sessions, I always believed it would be you, Erin." Ashley hugged her sister. "The one to make the family name proud."

"Really?" Erin sounded surprised.

Ashley nodded. "Absolutely. You're kind and you read a lot. What's not to like." Ashley tried to wink at her little sister, but instead, both eyes closed for a second. "Also, you're a Baxter. And that has to count for something in this competition."

In the car, after the celebrations for Erin calmed down, Ashley opened her sketchbook and drew one of her favorite drawings. Erin standing on a podium, award in hand. And nearby, Ashley and her siblings cheering her on. It was the most perfect day after all. Not only was the blizzard under way.

But a Baxter had finally won a character award.

16

Peace over Panic

KARI

Kari was so proud of Erin.

Finally, someone in the Baxter family had won a character award, and who better than the youngest of the four sisters? The smile on Erin's face as Mom drove them home from school was almost as wonderful as the snow pouring down around them.

Already the roads were hard to see.

"Take it slow, Mom." Ashley leaned forward, pressing against her seatbelt. "You don't want to get us stuck out here in the wilderness."

Brooke was in the front passenger seat. She looked back at Ashley. "We're on Main Street. It's not the wilderness."

231

"It's about to be." Ashley looked nervous. Like when she thought they were doing a five-day race instead of a 5K race last fall.

Just then an alarm sound interrupted the song on the radio, and a man's voice came on. "This is a message from the Emergency Broadcasting System." He sounded very serious.

The entire car grew quiet as the announcement continued. Mom turned the sound up.

"A major blizzard is hitting Indiana this afternoon and tonight. It is expected to release record amounts of snow across Bloomington and surrounding areas. Please take cover in the coming hours, and do not plan to leave home for several days as the roads will not be safe." There was another long alarm sound. "Again, this is a message from the Emergency Broadcasting System."

Mom turned the radio off and looked in the rearview mirror. "There you have it. The almanac was right."

"Do we have time to get home?" Ashley grabbed the passenger seat in front of her. "Or should we park here and make a snow fort to take cover in?"

"We have time to make it home, Ashley." Mom smiled. Her voice was calm. A good sign.

Kari settled back into her seat. The snow was falling harder now. "It won't be long, right?" She leaned forward and tapped their mother's shoulder. "Till we're home? It's getting really bad out here."

"Actually . . ." Mom turned the van into the parking lot of their favorite grocery store. "We need a few things before we go home." She parked the car and looked back at the five of them. "It'll be okay. I promise."

Brooke nodded. "Mom's right. We have time."

"And if we don't . . ." Luke sounded discouraged from the backseat. "At least we'll have an adventure. Since now I have to miss the Globetrotters!"

Kari looked at her brother. "I'm sorry about your field trip."

Mom glanced in the rearview mirror. "Luke. The school will probably reschedule. And if the roads are that bad, the basketball players wouldn't make it to town anyway."

"And we can build a fort in the living room!" Brooke looked back at their brother. "It'll be so fun!"

For the first time since they got in the van, Luke smiled. "Okay. I like that idea."

Kari really admired Brooke. As the oldest, she knew how to lead. And how to help the siblings feel better when they were down.

They all piled out of the van. The chill in the air was worse than it had been at school and it was hard to see through the thick falling snow. Kari tugged her jacket tight around her face and hurried along with her family toward the store.

But they weren't the only ones hurrying. Many people were darting in and out of the supermarket doors. And cars honked in the parking lot. Like everyone was in a panic to get what they needed before they couldn't get out of the house.

"Is Dad meeting us here?" Kari was worried. "There's certainly a lot of commotion."

"Your father will be home after work," Mom explained.

As they entered the store, Kari looked around. The lines were way longer than usual, and the workers behind the checkout counters were moving their hands faster than Kari had ever seen.

Once Mom grabbed a cart, she and Kari and the others marched toward the bread aisle.

"Bread is a good staple for snow." Mom walked with a pep in her step. "We could do toast or grilled cheese. Peanut butter and jelly sandwiches."

"Those are great options." Kari held on to the side of the cart. But she felt like she was being pulled along. "Mom. You're walking fast."

"Sorry, Kari." Mom didn't actually slow down. "I want to get home as soon as we can."

They rounded the corner for the bread aisle, and Kari felt her eyes get big. The shelves were almost empty. Where there usually were dozens and dozens of loaves of bread, now there were barely any.

"Hey!" Ashley shouted. "Someone stole all the bread!"

"No, Ashley." Brooke laughed. "It's just the snow. Everyone wants food all at once."

"Yes." Mom searched through the few loaves that remained. "This happens before a storm. People buy too much . . . because they panic."

"Here." Erin held up a loaf of wheat bread. "What about this?"

Ashley wrinkled her nose. "Wheat bread might as well be called brown cardboard."

Mom took the bread and placed it in the cart. "Yes, well . . . when the options are low, we just stay thankful."

Brooke grabbed a bag of tortillas from the end of the rack. "We could use these?"

Mom nodded, placing the bag in the cart. "That's the spirit. Now. To the milk and eggs!" She pointed ahead and continued the fast parade of Baxters through the market.

"Mom?" Kari ran alongside her.

"Yes, dear?" Mom stared ahead, dodging other customers on the way to the eggs.

"Why would people panic? Over a snowstorm?" Kari didn't understand. Why would anyone get upset with such good news on the horizon?

"Well. Some people don't feel ready. They want to have everything planned out. And when people aren't sure if they'll be snowed in one day, or three, or five, they start to worry and want to have whatever they think they may need. Sometimes more than they need." Mom looked at Kari as she race-walked. "In a moment of panic, it's sometimes hard to think clearly."

Ashley caught up with Kari and Mom and the others just as they got to the eggs. "Hey. I have an idea." Ashley raised both hands. "Maybe we should just get chickens."

"Yes. I am planning to buy *frozen* chicken." Mom pulled open the large fridge door that held all the cartons of eggs. "And two dozen of these."

"No, no, no." Ashley hopped up onto the back of the cart. "Real chickens. Then they can lay eggs for us. I also thought if you bought a cow for milk, we could save time trying to find the right supplies."

"That's very resourceful of you." Mom grabbed two egg cartons. "Please get off the cart."

Ashley hopped off. "Yes, ma'am."

Kari was enjoying this exchange between her sister and Mom. It was fun picturing chickens in the living room and a cow out back.

"This grocery store doesn't sell chickens or cows. That's what a farm is for." Mom looked up at the clock on the wall. "And the farms are most likely closed. So . . . we will have to stick with the store-bought eggs and milk."

Ashley didn't seem to want to give up on the topic. "What about vegetables?" She skipped along beside their mom. "We could grow a garden."

"Yes!" Kari took up the other side of the cart. Luke and Erin and Brooke hurried along behind them. "You do have a garden! It's perfect."

Mom placed the eggs into the cart. "Girls. Seeds can't grow in the winter. They need warmth and water and sun. There is no time for gardening. The blizzard is hitting us now."

"She has a point." Luke nodded.

"I agree." Erin looked nervous. "We need to get home."

"I second that." Brooke put her hands on her hips. "Enough talk about cows and chickens and vegetable gardens."

Ashley took a bow. "That part of my show is over. But I am available for farming in the future."

"Thank you, Ashley." Mom laughed.

And so they marched on.

Down to the milk and up to the cereal and over

to the fruit and veggies and around to the cheeses. Kari was certain that they covered every inch of the store.

"Whew." Ashley wiped her forehead. "This girl is exhausted."

Mom and Brooke and Erin and Luke stepped into a nearby aisle to find crackers. Kari and Ashley stayed on the main aisle with the cart. Kari looked around. "I hope all these people get everything they need."

"You're right." Ashley gasped. She cupped her hands around her mouth. "Attention!" she yelled. "Attention, shoppers!"

"Ashley!" Kari put her hand over her face. Mom wasn't going to like this.

"They have to know." Again, Ashley shouted. "An emergency is under way! Many of the shelves are empty! There will soon be no food. Not for weeks and weeks. So stock up!"

People were staring. Some glared at Ashley. Others hurried even more. And some just passed by, unfazed by the whole ordeal.

Mom and their three other siblings were hurrying back now. Mom didn't look happy.

"Ashley! You're making a scene." Mom pointed to the spot beside her. "Come here."

Ashley did as she was told.

"Not another word." Mom wasn't angry. Just serious. Kari could see that now.

"Yes, ma'am." Ashley's eyes looked sorry. "Not another word."

But as the family kept walking, Kari saw Ashley nodding at people, and silently gesturing toward the empty shelves.

Finally their mother noticed. "Ashley." Her tone was more serious. "Don't make people panic more than they already are."

"Okay." Ashley lifted her chin. "But I will have to live with myself for not saying more. Warnings are critical at a time like this, Mother."

"Everyone knows about the blizzard, Ashley. No need to warn them." Mom's hair hung in her face a little. She looked frazzled and Kari felt sorry for her. It was a lot of work getting blizzard food for a whole family.

They waited in a long checkout line and after

what felt like two hours, they trudged outside and into the snow. It was piling up fast. "Is . . . it safe?" Kari kicked at the snow as they walked back to the van.

"Yes." Mom smiled. But her teeth were chattering and she didn't look as sure as she had earlier. "Everything will be fine."

They had to drive very slow, but eventually they got home. Kari felt like she could breathe better as soon as they pulled into the driveway.

"Remember how we talked about panic back at the grocery store?" Mom turned the music down as she made her way toward the house.

"Yes." Luke nodded. "You said everyone was overbuying and stressed."

"Exactly. But in times like this, I'm reminded of God's peace." Mom took a deep breath. "Peace that helped me drive through the blizzard without feeling afraid."

"There wasn't much peace at the store." Brooke crossed her arms.

Mom parked the car. "Peace is a promise from God." She turned to the other kids, in the back of the car. "So, when we choose to trust God, we can feel peace. Even in the middle of a storm. We can experience peace over panic."

Ashley groaned from her seat in the car. "Even when there's no white bread." This caused a round of laughter from everyone.

"Even then, Ashley." Mom safely parked in the garage.

Kari thought about that for a moment and she realized that Mom was right. Panic could be a scary feeling. Like when they found out their family was moving from Ann Arbor to Bloomington. Or when Kari had to compete for the swim team. Those meets always made her antsy and sickish. But she could remember asking God for help in those moments.

And His help always would come. Maybe a friend would encourage her, or she would be able to take a deep breath, or she would just remember that God was with her.

Talking about this was a good reminder to Kari. God was a very real help in times of panic.

Once they had brought the groceries inside, Kari

and her siblings sat around the table. Those who had homework decided to get it done. Because if it did snow, then practicing spelling words or working on math equations was the last thing they'd want to do.

"Incredulous. I-N-C-R-E-D-U-L-O-U-S." Ashley spoke out loud as she practiced writing out the words assigned.

"What does that mean?" Luke was working on addition. Although he seemed more interested in what everyone else was doing.

"Um . . . It says skeptical or unbelieving." Ashley pushed back from the table and went to the window. "But it sounds like something that's incredibly ridiculous."

"Oh, like a mashed-up word." Luke grinned.

"Right." Ashley rested her forehead against the window. "Like. It's incredulous that it's snowing so hard already and Dad's not even home yet but that doesn't mean I will panic." She grabbed a very fast breath. "That sentence was a lot of words."

Sometimes Kari liked just watching Ashley.

Seeing what she was going to do next.

Mom poked her head out from the open refrigerator. "Ashley. Homework, please." Mom was still putting away groceries.

"Yes, Mom. But it is incredibly ridiculous." Ashley groaned and shuffled back to the table.

Kari went to her backpack and grabbed her journal. Ms. Nan had said it seemed silly to assign anything when there was snow in the forecast. So Kari decided to spend this time journaling. She opened her book to a blank page.

Hello! It's me, Kari. It's snowing so hard, I can't even believe it. But Dad's not home yet, and that makes me a little afraid. People keep saying this will be the biggest storm Bloomington has seen in years. Which makes me a little nervous. I hope I get to see a lot of snow. But I also don't want the house to be buried. Because then we would be stranded without enough food and stuck inside this house forever. But God, I know that You give us peace over panic. So, help me to trust You and not to worry. I know this storm will be fun. I just hope Dad gets back soon. Also, tomorrow, I really want to sled. That's all for now. Talk soon, Kari.

Waiting for Dad

ASHLEY

Ashley couldn't get anything done.

She tried to finish the take-home packet that Ms. Stritch had handed out but it was no use. Every five seconds her attention turned to the window and the snow piling up outside. Ashley walked to the back door and cracked it open. A blast of snow covered her face and took her breath. "I really think it might snow forever."

She slammed the door. "Dad is definitely not out there."

"Ashley." Mom sounded firm. "Of course he's not out there. He's at the hospital, where he should be. Working." She sighed. "Please. Do your spelling."

Ashley spun around. This was the third time

Mom had asked Ashley to sit down. "Very well, Mother." Ashley could sense she was on the very thinnest of ice. "I will commit to doing my homework."

No one wanted to start a big snow week in trouble.

"What if Dad is stuck on a road somewhere?" Erin didn't look up from the book she was buried in.

"I will say"—Ashley was back in her seat at the table—"now is not the time for losing our dad. Maybe we should bundle up and go look for him!" Ashley looked back at Mom. "What do ya say, Mother?"

Mom didn't say anything.

"I'm worried about him." Luke bit his lip. "He should be here."

"You're right." Mom looked at the clock. "He should be here very soon. But we will not go out in the snow to look for him." She raised her eyebrows at Ashley. "Do you understand?"

Ashley glanced at the door for a few seconds. Then she hurried her answer. "Yes. I do understand. No rescue missions."

"Not yet, anyway," Kari whispered. She tapped her fingers on the kitchen table.

Their mother didn't hear that last part, apparently. Because she smiled at them and headed for the stairs. "I'm going to check the basement for flashlights and bottled water," she told them. "I'll be right back up."

When she was gone, Brooke set her pencil down. "I can't finish these." She had been going over history questions. "I miss Dad."

Erin stood and paced a bit. "Do you think that maybe . . . he's stranded?"

"No. No way." Brooke crossed her arms. "He probably just got behind. Dad would never get stranded."

"But Erin has a point." Kari looked worried. "Maybe he needs help."

Suddenly, Ashley knew what to do. "Okay. The snow is about to bury the door and then we'll have no way out. Everyone get your coats and meet at the back door. We have to find Dad."

"Ashley, that's ridiculous." Brooke frowned. "Besides, Mom would never let us go."

"True." Ashley tapped her chin. "Meet at the *front* door." She hurried upstairs and her siblings followed.

Brooke caught up to Ashley. "I'm staying inside. It's too cold."

"That's fine with me." Ashley's courage was at an all-time high.

She reached her bedroom, and Kari already had not one, but two coats on. "We can start down the driveway and turn left." Kari slipped on her boots. "Does that sound right?"

"Yes. And then just keep walking." Ashley put on her heavy coat and a beanie. And then another pair of sweatpants plus her rubber boots and her gloves. Suddenly she was very hot. "It's kinda hard to breathe with all this on."

"You'll be glad you have it when we get to the hospital. It's far away." Kari looked afraid. "All I know is we need to find him. I'll be downstairs." Kari ran out of the room.

Ashley grabbed one last item, an oversized red scarf. She glanced at herself in the mirror. She was nearly unrecognizable. But at least she would be safe from the blizzard. Ashley hobbled down the stairs, where she met her siblings, all bundled up and ready to go.

"All right. Everyone follow my lead," Ashley whispered. She turned the lock and the handle and opened the front door with caution. *Squeeeeeaaaak!* The door was not quiet. Ashley winced and closed her eyes.

"Hurry," Erin whispered.

Ashley opened the door the rest of the way and ushered her siblings out one by one into the snowstorm. They wobbled down the steps and toward the driveway, their boots sinking in the deep snow.

Ashley went last. As she turned to shut the door she heard Mom's voice.

"What in the world is happening here?" She sounded frantic.

The jig was up. Ashley turned back toward her siblings. "Hey, everyone, come inside! It's time for dinner!"

Mom gave her a look. "This was your idea, wasn't it?"

"Someone had to think about our dad." Ashley felt her shoulders slump deep inside the jackets. "I'm sorry. We should've asked first."

The others were back at the porch now. All of them covered in snow.

When they were back inside, Mom helped them remove their coats and extra jeans and sweats. "Kids. Don't ever leave without asking." She seemed to be recovering from the shock. "Dad will be fine. The roads are still drivable."

"Can we pray for him?" Erin seemed hopeful at the idea.

"Yes, Erin." Mom nodded. "I like that." They all formed a circle and held hands. Mom said the prayer. "Lord, we ask You to keep Dad safe on the road. Please help him to get home soon, and give us a special time during this blizzard. And please help us remember that peace is better than panic. In Jesus's name, amen."

Just at that moment, they heard the garage door opening.

"Dad's home!" Erin shouted.

Luke clapped. "Yes!"

"Great. Now let's see how quickly we can put these coats away!" Mom gestured upstairs. "Go go go!"

Ashley and her siblings darted up the stairs, laughing and celebrating, their arms full of coats. Because Dad was home and that meant now they were all together.

Ashley put away her clothes and walked to the

window. The snow was even harder now.

"You coming downstairs, Ash?" Kari finished hanging her coat.

"Not yet." Ashley faced her sister. "You go ahead. I'll be down in a few minutes."

"Okay!" Kari skipped out of the room.

Ashley shut off their bedroom light, so that the only brightness in the room was a teddy bear lamp that gave off a slightly yellow color. Ashley grabbed her sketchbook and sat on the floor.

She drew her siblings bundled up to go rescue Dad. She giggled thinking about how silly they must have looked.

Mid-drawing, Ashley went to her window again. The snow was falling so fast it looked like confetti. She stood there for a moment just taking it in. Then she returned to her sketch.

She added snowflakes—every shape and size. There. That was enough. One last time she stared out her bedroom window. The sight was . . . well, it was incredulous.

Ashley could hear the mumbled voices of her

family downstairs, and she would join them soon enough. But she didn't want to rush this moment. This perfect, exciting, snowy moment. The blizzard was finally here.

She could hardly believe it.

Albert the Snowman

KARI

The blizzard blasted Bloomington harder than Kari could have dreamed.

She woke up Tuesday morning and ran to the window. Snow was still coming down. Everywhere she looked. The world was covered in white in every direction. A blanket of snow so bright, it was hard to look at.

Last night before they went to bed, they ran to the front to measure just how high the snow was. Under the snowy night sky, they had trudged out to the front yard in their snow boots and, using Dad's tape measure, they were able to see that it had snowed around six inches. Luke had reminded everyone that six inches was half a ruler.

The snow kept falling on their nighttime snow adventure, but that hadn't stopped the Baxter kids. They had a snowball fight in the front yard as the blizzard blew snow all around. The thick drifts made their voices and laughter sound muted. As if they were in their own snow globe. The family soon ran inside, their fingers too frozen to stay in the snow any longer. They sat by the fire for a while and then they went to bed.

Kari and Ashley both had trouble falling asleep. The snow was too exciting.

The memory from last night faded and Kari grabbed a nearby blanket and put it around her shoulders. Just looking at the falling snow made her cold. She tucked her knees under her and smiled, taking in the blizzard for another few moments. Bo hopped up on the window bench and snuggled with her.

"Isn't it the most amazing thing you've ever seen?" Kari whispered to the pup. The snow had probably at least doubled since last night. And Kari couldn't wait to get out and play.

If only her siblings would wake up.

She could hear someone in the kitchen, so Kari put on her robe and slippers and padded down the stairs. There she found their mom, pulling together the ingredients for cinnamon rolls.

"Wanna help?" Mom smiled at her. She kept her voice low because the others were still asleep.

"Yes, please!" Kari rolled up her sleeves.

She and Mom worked together to roll the dough and add the cinnamon and butter and sugar. They had the best time. "They look pretty great!" Her mother stepped back and surveyed their work.

"Better than cannolis!" Kari helped glaze the rolls, then Mom slid the tray into the oven.

Just then, Dad came through the garage door into the house. He was holding a stack of wood. He looked tired.

"Woo." Dad set the wood by the fireplace. "It's still coming down."

"Why didn't you come through the back door?" Kari sat up.

Dad laughed. "That door is blocked with snow. There's no easy path in."

"No way!" Kari gasped. She stood and hurried

for the door. She pulled up the blinds and sure enough, she could see through the glass door how high the snow was. It was higher than her waist. Dad was right. There was no way that door could be opened.

"See." Dad walked over. "Snow much fun."

Kari laughed. "That's a good one, Dad."

"Coffee?" Mom walked over with a mug and handed it to Dad.

"Thank you." He took a sip. "Ah. So warm." Dad cupped the mug in his hands.

"I love the snow." Mom looked out the back door. "Do we have enough wood in the shed?"

Dad nodded. "I think so. I grabbed what was left. They think we'll lose power this afternoon."

"Lose power?" Kari frowned. "What does that mean?"

Dad smiled and patted Kari's back. "It means we may be in for an adventure."

"That's why Dad got the firewood," Mom chimed in.

"Morning." Ashley skipped into the kitchen, a wide smile across her face. She was dressed in her snow gear. "I heard someone say 'adventure.'"

"Morning." Kari motioned to the back door. "We can't get out. Too much snow."

"We can get out." Dad smiled. "But we have to go through the garage."

"Good thing." Ashley plopped to the floor and slid her boots on. "I want to get out in that stuff right now. It's not every day that you survive a blizzard."

"She has a point." Kari leaned against the kitchen counter and stared at the oven. Already the cinnamon rolls were spreading out across the tray.

"Yeah, well . . . The snow won't wait. I don't want it to melt." Ashley hopped to her feet and pulled a beanie over her head. She took the beanie off again. "But I should probably eat first."

They all laughed, and one at a time the others joined them until all seven of them were together. Mom brought a plate of eggs and a tray of the cinnamon rolls to the table. "You have time for the snow. It's not going anywhere for a while."

"This is the best morning." Luke jumped in place a few times. "Look at all that snow!"

"The best!" Erin took a seat at the kitchen table. "We gotta go outside after we eat!"

Once everyone saw what breakfast was, it wasn't hard to convince them to eat. Kari shared a smile with Mom. After all, they were the chefs on this snowy day. Dad said a prayer and they all ate as fast as possible. Everyone wanted to be outside.

And soon enough they were.

Everyone got to work right away on a snowman. Mom and Brooke went back inside to find items for the snowman itself. And the others all brought handfuls of snow together, working on the base. Kari patted the snow down so it would stick. She stepped back and examined her work. The base was becoming a nice round boulder.

"It's looking good!" Dad nodded. "An old-fashioned snowman."

"It's gonna be the best snowman ever." Luke brought an armful of snow and added it to the base.

"We should name him something." Ashley was throwing snowballs for Bo to catch. Only, he never caught them. He just rubbed his nose in the snow looking for the ball, which had disappeared in the mound of snow.

"You think he gets cold?" Kari was concerned about their dog.

"Nah!" Dad shook his head. "He loves it out here."

Bo hopped in and out of the snowbanks, sniffing and panting. Dad was right. Bo seemed to enjoy the snow just as much as everyone else did.

Dad pointed to the snowman. "Kari, why don't you and Ashley start on the snowman's midsection."

Kari got to her knees and started to make a smaller round ball for the middle of the man. "So what do we name him?"

"Maybe Albert." Ashley walked over to Kari. "Or Ronnie."

Kari laughed. "Those seem like perfect snowman names."

Mom and Brooke brought the accessories from inside. Mom dropped a load of clothing near the snowman. "Here's that top hat from the costume box. And I found a scarf." She squealed, making her way over to the snowman. "It's freezing out here."

Brooke held up a shoebox. "And I brought a few pieces of coal from the grill out back and a carrot." She spread them out on the snow.

By now, Kari and Ashley were done with their parts and Luke and Erin and Dad finished up the head. He was becoming a beautiful snowman.

Luke put his arm around Ashley. "So . . . is he Albert?"

"Well . . ." Ashley looked at Kari. "What do you think?"

"Yes. Albert is perfect." Kari clapped her hands. "But he does need eyes and a nose."

Brooke and Mom pressed the coal for eyes onto Albert's face. And Mom lifted Erin so she could give him a carrot nose.

Dad walked over to Kari. "Kari. How about you get the hat?"

Kari's face lit up. "Okay."

Dad helped her up and placed her on his shoulders. Mom handed Kari the big black top hat and Kari placed it on top of Albert. The finishing touch. Dad let Kari down from his shoulders and they all stepped back and observed the snowman. Albert had a crooked smile and the carrot nose was skinny. He stood tall and straight. Very handsome, as snowmen go.

"Albert Baxter," Kari said out loud. "He's perfect."

"Now . . . how about we go for a—" Dad didn't get to finish his sentence. A snowball hit him right in the chest.

"Got ya!" Luke's voice echoed through the front yard.

And with that, the family all began one huge snowball fight. Kari worked her fastest to make a few snowballs, then she threw them at everyone she could. Everyone laughed and chased one another in circles. Kari got tired real fast. She plopped down on the snow and looked up at the gray sky.

It was still snowing!

"Snow angels!" Erin joined Kari.

"Great idea!" Brooke followed. And then Ashley and Luke and finally Mom and Dad until the whole family was doing snow angels.

"Albert the snowman was a jolly happy soul!" Ashley started her own rendition of the Frosty song. And, in Ashley fashion, she got everyone on board. They worked on their snow angels, taking turns to make up new lyrics that applied to Albert.

Laying on the ground with her family, Kari remembered the meteor shower, and how they had all stargazed together that night. Only now they were snow gazing. All together in one moment enjoying their time and the wonderful wintery world around them. Kari smiled and closed her eyes. Thank You, God, for this beautiful blizzard and for my family. Snowflakes fell on her face and as she opened her eyes, she saw everyone walking for the front door. It was time to go inside, time to get warm.

But like the night of the meteor shower, this snowy blizzard morning was one Kari would remember forever.

Later in the afternoon everyone sat together relaxing, enjoying the bliss of having nothing to do and nowhere to go.

Kari turned to look at Erin. "I'm still so proud of you for your character award."

"Thanks, Kari." Erin sighed. "It was such a great feeling. For what it's worth, you all deserved an award."

"I agree." Ashley sketched on the floor. "But sometimes you can't get what you want."

"That's growth." Kari was impressed. "Coming from the instructor herself."

"We did our best." Ashley smiled. "And that's all we can do."

"You are all award winners to me." Mom flipped through a magazine on the couch.

Kari thought that it was so sweet to hear Mom say that. To feel supported and cheered on by her family was amazing. Then—just like her dad had predicted—the entire house went dark. Dark and silent.

"There goes the power." Mom looked to their father. "You said it would happen."

"The power lines can only take so much snow." Dad looked around at Kari and her siblings. "Don't worry, kids. This is just part of a big blizzard."

"What do we do now?" Ashley ducked her head under a blanket. "Help!"

Luke laughed. "You're so funny, Ashley!"

"I'm with Ashley. This is scary." Erin found a blanket from the couch and covered herself up in it.

"No need to panic." Dad stayed in his chair. "We have enough firewood and food. We will be okay."

"John, why don't you start a fire in the fireplace." Mom got up from the couch. "I should make sandwiches before it gets too dark." She walked into the kitchen.

"I'm still scared." Erin clearly did not like this.

"We have each other." Kari tried to encourage her youngest sister. "Like Dad said, we'll be fine."

"Wait here." Brooke ran to the cupboards near the TV and pulled out blankets and pillows. "Living room fort time?"

"Yes! Good idea." Luke hopped off the couch and ran upstairs. "I'll get more blankets."

"Erin, help me with this." Brooke tossed the blankets and pillows on the floor.

Kari and the others joined to create an entrance

and exit and giving the blanket fort some height. They used pillows and couch cushions and after half an hour, they had a Baxter family fort, right there in the living room.

About that time, Mom walked into the living room.

"I thought I had tons of canned food. Tuna and vegetables and fruits." She looked confused. "But, I can't find anything." She put her hands on her hips. "I have no idea where they went."

"It worked." Ashley clapped and jumped to her feet. "Hang on." She sprinted out of the room.

Mom looked at Kari. "You know about this?"

"No." Kari shook her head. "No idea."

Ashley returned with an armful of cans. "Ta-da!"

"Ta-da?" Mom took half of the cans from Ashley's armful. "What's all this?"

"When I heard about the blizzard, I started a safety stash." Ashley beamed with pride. "In case we needed them. And we did. And there's lots more where those came from." She paused. "You're welcome."

"Well . . . the pantry is a fine place for cans. But

thank you for helping." Mom let out a laugh. Like she couldn't help herself. "I'll get some tuna sandwiches started." She returned to the kitchen.

"I'll get the flashlights." Dad headed out of the living room.

"Let's go into the fort!" Kari led the way through the blanket entrance. Pillows stacked up five high to make up the walls, and a big blanket served as the roof. It was the biggest fort they had ever built. There was a spot for everyone to sit, so all five Baxter children found a place.

"I like us." Erin wrapped a blanket around her shoulders.

"Me, too." Brooke put her arm around Erin.

"You know." Ashley was on her stomach, clutching a pillow. "We have a lot of fun together. Not every family could make a snowman, have a snowball fight, and build a living room fort. All in one day."

After a few minutes, Mom poked her head into the fort. "Early dinner is served!" She entered the tent holding a tray of sandwiches and a bowl of apple slices.

"The light man is here." Dad followed behind her with two lantern-style flashlights and an armful of smaller ones.

"What if the batteries run out?" Erin sounded scared.

"We have more." Dad crawled into the living room fort and found a spot with them.

Mom did the same. "Oooh, it's cozy in here."

Dad adjusted the flashlight lantern so it became brighter. "The thing with darkness is it only takes a little bit of light . . ." He twisted a knob on the lantern. "To change everything."

The glow of the lantern lit up the place. The quilts they had hung up, with their patches of red, and blue and pink, looked beautiful in this lighting.

"Wow. You really are the light man." Luke's jaw hung open.

Mom held up a book. "Narnia. *The Lion, the Witch and the Wardrobe.* What do you say?"

"Yes! It's perfect for a snow day." Kari moved over so she could sit next to Mom. She liked to follow along while Mom read out loud. For the next several hours Mom read about the children

269

and their discovery of a magical wardrobe that took them to the snowy land of Narnia, where it was always winter, and the White Witch was in charge.

Kari had heard this story before, so she knew how it ended. She closed her eyes and leaned against Mom's shoulder.

Between her full belly and Mom's calming voice, Kari was cozy enough to almost fall asleep. There was nothing like the sound of their mother reading out loud.

Darkness settled over the house and the snow kept falling.

They left the fort and ate more sandwiches, all of them cuddled on the couch and chairs near the fireplace.

"We can all sleep in here tonight," Dad announced.

Everyone was too tired to cheer, but Kari could see that each of her siblings was smiling.

Mom read another book—*Little House on the Prairie*—and Kari felt her eyes grow heavy. This time, she didn't fight sleep. She felt safe and warm and cozy with her family all around her. One by one, everyone found a spot in the fort or on the floor, comfy in the blankets and pillows, and soon the Baxter children were all falling asleep.

Their parents, too.

Nothing in all of life was better than this blizzard sleepover in the glow of the fireplace. If Kari had the choice to go to dance class tonight, or see Mandy and Liza, or go on a field trip to the moon, she would politely say, "No, thank you."

Because right here was exactly where Kari Baxter wanted to be.

19

Being Baxters

ASHLEY

*C*runch, crunch, crunch!

The sound of her boots in the snow had become Ashley's favorite in the whole wide world. At least for this week. It was Friday morning and the Baxters were out sledding. Which was a particularly fun activity because of not only the rush of flying down the hill, but also the adventure of walking back up.

The snow had begun to melt, but you couldn't really tell. The world was still covered in white.

"Yahooo!" Luke flew past Ashley. He was belly first on his sled.

"Go, Luke!" Ashley turned around, pumping her fists in the air. She watched her brother make his way down the rest of the hill. At the bottom, parents and non-sledders cheered and clapped. A lot of people from the area were on the hill today. Ashley didn't know all of them, but she was happy to see the Howard family. They were the neighbors down the street.

Bloomington had some very friendly people. Ashley was glad this was her home.

As she pulled her sled behind her, up the steep hill for the sixth time in a row that morning, Ashley thought about this past week they'd spent as a family and how fast it had gone.

Once the power returned, the next day around lunchtime, everyone felt relieved. After all, they didn't want the food in the fridge to spoil. And they couldn't bear to eat cold canned goods for much longer.

Ashley had been the first to admit that her stash was useful, but not tasty.

In the days since the power came back on, the Baxters continued to make the most fun memories. They watched movies including Ashley's favorite, *The Lion King*. She loved the music and the silly characters. But this time while watching it, Ashley changed the lyrics to "I just can't wait to be *queen*." Since she was a queen in the making. And she even wore her cardboard crown all of that day.

Of course, they had to make a few of Mom's special winter recipes. Like cookie bars and taco salad and peanut butter balls. They played games. Spoons was a popular one. The rules were easy, but the competition was tough. Several spoons were yanked and, if the family didn't love each other so much, there may have been more arguing. But ultimately, every game they played turned into laughter and added another memory to their hearts.

Ashley reached the top of the hill and exhaled. "Whew! It sure is pretty. But man is it a workout." She put her hands over her head and took some deep breaths.

"We're definitely building up an appetite." Kari walked over to where Ashley caught her breath. "I think Mom is making pancakes later."

"Breakfast for lunch is always a good idea." Ashley picked up her sled. "Wanna go double?"

"Yes!" Kari tightened her gloves. "Bring it on."

"All right. Squeeze in." Ashley laid the sled down and took a spot at the back, making room for Kari in the front. "Adventure awaits!"

Kari sat in front of Ashley. "Adventure awaits!"

"One, two, three, go!" Ashley used her arms to push the sled toward the sloped part of the hill. The sliding became faster and faster and within seconds, Ashley and Kari whooshed down the hill. They laughed and screamed as snow flew into their faces. The sled turned sideways and tipped the girls out. Ashley and Kari rolled down the hill three times until they reached the bottom.

When she'd stopped rolling, Ashley sat up. She couldn't stop laughing. She looked over at Kari, who had a face full of snow.

"Oh no!" Ashley crawled over to Kari. "Here, let me help you!" Ashley removed her gloves and brushed the snow off Kari's cheeks and nose.

"You're rubbing it in!" Kari laughed. "Burrrrr!"

Ashley breathed into her hands. "I'm freezing!"

Dad ran to the two girls. "That was quite the tumble." He helped them both to their feet.

"We were almost buried in snow." As Ashley

stood, she felt the snow slipping down her back. "It's in my jacket."

"And all over my face!" Kari blew out several times. She giggled. By now, Mom, Erin, Brooke and Luke were standing nearby.

Ashley shook her head and bent over, letting the snow that hadn't melted yet fall off her. "I am officially a snow-girl."

"And I'm cold." Erin crossed her arms.

"We're all cold." Luke scooped snow up and tossed it in the air. "I love it!" Some of the snow fell into Brooke's coat.

She gasped. "Luke!" Brooke grabbed some snow and threw it at him.

"All right, Brooke!" Luke smiled. "That's it!" Luke grabbed a snowball and chased Brooke down the snow-covered road.

"No!" Brooke laughed and screamed, running ahead of Luke.

"Okay." Mom looped her arm through Dad's. "Let's go make those pancakes."

"Good idea." Dad smiled. They led the way back to the house.

Ashley went last and she was sure to leave plenty of space in between her and the family. Because, selfishly, she wanted to hear the crunch of her boots in the snow one more time.

Crunch, crunch, crunch!

Evening came too fast, which often happened this blizzard week. As they finished up the last of the leftover taco salad, they played another round of the question game, which led to more laughter and stories.

"We should do this when we get back to school. Like invite friends over for taco salad and play the question game." Brooke sipped her water.

"You mean have leftovers on purpose?" Mom chuckled. "Wouldn't your friends want fresh food?"

"Not when leftovers are as good as yours." Luke scarfed down another forkful of his dinner.

"And the question game never gets old." Kari rubbed her hands together. Ashley assumed she was still cold.

"They always make me laugh." Erin stretched.

"Especially when Mom asks questions."

"Me? I'm very serious," Mom teased as she finished up her food.

"Yeah. Like the question about whether you'd want a beak or a trunk." Luke shook his head.

"Okay, so a little fun never hurt." Mom winked.

"I love our question game." Dad smiled. "It's special."

"Laughter and leftovers," Ashley blurted out.

"What?" Dad looked confused.

Ashley went on. "We could have friends come over and call it *Laughter and Leftovers*." Ashley looked around the table. "It sounds pretty good to me." She was proud of herself.

"I like it." Mom nodded. "Let's do it. When the roads are clear, we can have our first Baxters' Laughter and Leftovers."

"Elizabeth. You think it's time for that thing I told you about?" Dad's eyes danced, the way they did when there was an exciting secret on the horizon.

"The thing?" Mom lifted her eyebrows, looking like she was playing along.

"What thing?" Brooke squealed.

"Honey! Come on." Dad stood and moved back from the table.

Mom joined him. "Okay! I'm excited." She clapped her hands.

"Living room!" Dad pointed and he and Mom hurried out of the dining area.

"Now?" Luke's eyes were wide.

"Now!" Mom called back as she followed Dad upstairs. "We'll meet you in the living room."

"I'm nervous . . ." Erin took a sip of water before leaving the table.

"Why?" Ashley slid back from the table. "I love a surprise!"

Erin walked along next to Ashley. "What if we're moving again?"

"We're not moving again, Erin," Brooke reassured the youngest Baxter girl.

Ashley put her arm around Erin. "And even if we were . . ."

"Which we're not!" Brooke reminded Erin again.

"But if we were . . . we'd be okay." Ashley looked around at her siblings. "We have been through it once. And we had each other. We still do. We can get through anything."

"Plus. Dad sounded too excited for it to be a bad surprise." Luke flopped on the couch.

"I guess you're right." Erin sat on the couch as well. She pulled her legs up and took a few deep breaths. "But maybe it's bad . . ."

"You worry too much, Erin." Brooke kept her tone kind. "It'll be fine." She dropped to the floor, cross-legged.

"Maybe we're going on a cruise! Like the Howards!" Kari took the last spot on the couch next to Luke, who was now sandwiched between Kari and Erin.

Ashley sat on the floor next to Brooke. "Give it up, Kari. There's no cruise." Kari had been wanting a cruise since their neighbors went. But their family wasn't going on one anytime soon. They learned how to have adventures in other ways.

"Maybe one day." Brooke looked back and smiled at Kari. Then she looked at Ashley. "Right, Ash?"

It was more important to be kind than to be

right. So, Ashley smiled at Kari. "Yeah. Maybe one day."

Just then, Dad and Mom hurried down the stairs and into the living room. They were out of breath and smiling. And Dad held something behind his back.

"Ready?" Mom looked over at Dad. He nodded.

"Are we moving?" Erin looked like she might cry.

"No. We're not moving." Dad laughed. "I know it's been a crazy few months. The science camp and dance classes and world fair and blizzard."

Mom continued. She looked at Erin and then Luke. "Getting glasses and a canceled field trip." Next their mother turned to Brooke. "Mean kids at school."

"And we are very proud of Erin for winning the character award at school. Give it up for Erin!" Dad led a round of applause and cheers.

Ashley turned back to Erin. Her sister smiled, the kind of shy smile that comes from someone who doesn't like attention. "Thanks, everyone."

Dad pulled a stack of papers from behind his

back. "But we thought there should be a few more character awards handed out." He held out the papers. "This is the First Annual Baxter Family Character Awards."

Ashley sat straight up. Her siblings did the same thing. This was the last thing they had expected.

Mom held up the first piece of paper. "First. For always being an encourager to his sisters, and for having a good attitude despite his field trip getting canceled, the *Most Positive* award goes to Luke Baxter!"

The family applauded and whooped and hollered as Luke left the couch and grabbed his certificate. Ashley could hardly believe this was happening. And with no school assembly at all.

Dad winked at Luke. "I heard the Globetrotters are rescheduling. So, guess who's going on a family adventure!" Dad pumped his fists with excitement.

"Really?" Luke shouted, high-fiving Dad. "All of us?"

"Yes!" Mom shouted back. "Dad is going to buy tickets for the rescheduled game in May. We're all going!"

The family burst into cheers and hugs. And, while Ashley still wasn't sure what these Globetrotters were all about, she was thrilled to be going. And more thrilled that Luke was going to get to see the game. Luke stared at his award as he walked back to his seat.

Dad stepped forward. "Next up. For being strong in the face of adversity, and making the best out of having to wear glasses, the *Most Resilient* award goes to our two-time award winner, Erin Baxter!"

Erin jumped up from her spot and rushed over to Dad and Mom. She wrapped her arms around them both. "Thank you, thank you, thank you!"

Mom looked at Kari. "This next award goes to someone who learned the hard way that it's better to share than to shine alone. And that being kind to others is better than being a star." Their mother smiled. "Tonight the *Share the Spotlight* award goes to Kari Baxter."

"Way to go, Kari!" Luke cheered.

Kari hurried over and grabbed her award from Mom. She hugged their parents for a while before returning to her spot.

Dad held up another sheet of paper. He looked right at Ashley. "A coach, a prepper and a leader. This next award goes to the Baxter who always has a plan. She is smart and brave, and she brings everyone together. The *Most Original* award goes to Ashley Baxter."

Butterflies danced in Ashley's stomach. Only they weren't the bad kind. They were the good kind. Like Samson the butterfly, her old friend from last year. Because one of her dreams was finally coming true. She stood and walked to her parents. She took her time.

"Here you go, my unique and incredible daughter." Dad handed Ashley the certificate. "I'm so proud to be your father."

Ashley stared at the award for a minute. Maybe five. She wasn't sure. But she wasn't in a hurry. The paper had beautiful gold trim and read: CHARACTER AWARD. Ashley ran her hand across it.

She felt tears in her eyes, happy ones.

"You okay?" Dad bent down and brushed a piece of hair off Ashley's forehead.

She looked up at him and whispered, "It's my

own character award. I wanted one for so long." She let out a relieved laugh.

Dad pulled her into a hug. "I know. And you earned it, honey." He kissed the top of her head.

Mom joined the hug. "You are an amazing Baxter daughter. And we are so glad you're ours."

Ashley sighed and wiped the tears from her eyes. "Very well. For my acceptance speech, I'd like to thank—"

"Ashley." Mom put her hand on Ashley's shoulder. "You don't have to give a speech."

"I kinda want to." Ashley took a deep breath. "If I may?"

"Okay." Her mom chuckled a bit. Then her dad did, too.

"Yes. Go ahead, honey." Dad reached for Mom's hand and they waited.

Ashley took her time. "First, I'd like to thank God. He gave me my unique self. And next I'd like to thank my family. And Principal Bond for not giving me a character award because this one means more now. And I'd like to thank Ms. Stritch for being so horrible to us so that I could learn how to make another unlikely friend. And each of my siblings for doing so well in our training sessions. And . . . that's it." Ashley walked back to her spot on the floor and took a seat. "Oh, and God save the Queen!" Her British accent made a reappearance, much to the delight of everyone in the room. "Me. I'm the Queen."

"Okay. Let's move on." Dad looked at Brooke. "Finally. This last Baxter has led her younger siblings well."

Their mom looked at their oldest sister, too. "She has navigated the pains of middle school, with grace and patience. And she is growing into a beautiful young woman, because of her big heart. The *Best Example* award goes to Brooke Baxter!"

Everyone cheered a final time as Brooke got her award. "Thank you." She smiled at their parents. "I don't have an acceptance speech." She grinned at Ashley. "But thank you."

When she sat back down again Dad looked at the kids once more.

"These last couple of months, your mom and I have seen you all handle tough things well. And there may be tough times ahead. That's life. But we know you will be okay. We know because you are part of this family. And being in this family means something."

Mom nodded. "It means you're honest. And patient. It means you lead more than you follow." Mom took time to look at each of the kids in the eyes. "You use a kind tone. You share. You represent God well and you represent all of us well. And that's what it means to be a Baxter."

Dad's face was full of love as he finished up. "We have been given so much by God. So much love and laughter and time together. We have food and clothing and shelter. The Bible says, to whom much is given, much will be expected. So, let's love well and laugh often."

"Yes." Mom grinned. "Let's look for the miraculous moments every day, because they are always happening around us." She paused. "And let's live our lives for God. That's what being Baxters means."

Ashley thought about those two words. *Being Baxters.* That was something she would remember forever.

The ceremony ended and after dinner that night, the family had another night of fun. Mom and Brooke made brownies. Luke and Dad and Erin played Battleship. Kari journaled on the floor.

But Ashley just closed her eyes and took it all in.

The quiet laughter and smell of chocolate. Bo's paws tapping across the wood floor. And the crackling fire Dad built before dinner.

She wanted to hold on to this moment forever.

She took a spot next to Kari on the floor. It was time for a new sketch. Only this time Ashley didn't draw it in her sketchbook. She drew it on the back of her character award.

Ashley sketched a picture of the whole family on the couch. They weren't doing anything silly or adventurous. There were no animals or goofy props, like a boa or a sash. They were just sitting together. Like they would do later that night when they watched a movie or when Mom read a book to them.

The drawing was perfect because it represented all that mattered to Ashley. Her whole world. And it represented something that would never change.

Cause the fact was, things would change. The snow would melt. They would have to go back to school. Ms. Stritch would have to leave once Mr. Garrett returned. Erin's glasses would become so normal no one would think twice about them. Kari would start dance classes up again. Bo would get older and never want to leave the living room.

And one day soon, when summer came, Ashley would leave fifth grade forever.

But right here, right now, all of that seemed like it would never happen. Like life would always stay like this and she would always be in fifth grade and the blizzard week would never end.

Ashley focused again on the laughter around her, and she remembered the meals around the table, the living room fort and their time making Albert the snowman. Every wonderful thing about this blizzard week.

If they could get through a faraway move from Ann Arbor to Bloomington . . . if they could survive making new friends, wild talent shows and science camp . . . and even this crazy blizzard, then with God, they could get through anything together.

Because that's what being Baxters really meant.
What it would always mean.

About the Authors

Karen Kingsbury, #1 *New York Times* bestselling novelist, is America's favorite inspirational story-teller, with more than twenty-five million of her award-winning books in print. Her last dozen titles have topped bestseller lists and many of her novels are under development as major motion pictures. Her Baxter Family books have been developed into a TV series slated to debut soon. Karen is also an adjunct professor of writing at Liberty University. She and her husband, Donald, live in Tennessee near their children and grandchildren.

Tyler Russell has been telling stories his whole life. In elementary school, he won a national award for a children's book he wrote. Since then, he hasn't stopped writing. In 2015, he graduated with a BFA from Lipscomb University. He sold his first screen-play, *Karen Kingsbury's Maggie's Christmas Miracle*, which premiered on Hallmark. Along with screen-plays and novels, Tyler is a songwriter, singer, actor, and creative who lives in Nashville, Tennessee.